The Daybreak Siege

When Abe Teegle and his gang hit a train, they didn't reckon upon troubleshooter Dan Dallobar being on board. Despite having been asleep, Dan was still able to wound one of the robbers during their escape and it wasn't long before the troubleshooter was deputed to hunt down the gang.

Meanwhile in a rancho on the borderlands, a crippled old Mexican don hatches plans to recover his stolen property.

It would all come together in a lawless town when a bloody shoot-out was fated to bring death to good and bad men alike. Only then would the terror end.

The Daybreak Siege

VIC J. HANSON

A Black Horse Western

ROBERT HALE · LONDON

© Vic J. Hanson 2001
First published in Great Britain 2001

ISBN 0 7090 6944 8

Robert Hale Limited
Clerkenwell House
Clerkenwell Green
London EC1R 0HT

Typeset by
Derek Doyle & Associates, Liverpool.
Printed and bound in Great Britain by
Antony Rowe Limited, Wiltshire

For Kerry, Gary, Martin, Garrie and Melanie

PART ONE

Rail-Raiders

ONE

They brought the powder-man in at the last minute, an oldster called merely the Miner because that was what he had been. He wasn't particularly brainy but very good at what he could do with high explosives.

Till it was time for him to be used he minded the horses in sight of the rail-line about a mile from the rising bend where the train had invariably to slow down.

There was a convenient outcrop of rocks a little ahead of the grove, and here the remaining four of the bunch crouched.

From the rocks the distance to the lines wasn't too much, and the snakelike train was crawling when it came abreast of the crouching men. They knew it would pick up speed, so they had to move fast.

One by one, at short intervals, they jumped on

9

the train. The Miner, with his accoutrements, was helped on last.

This was the end of the train. There were a few staring faces; curious, that was all, so it seemed.

The gang didn't have their guns out yet. Nobody spoke to them.

The dispatch car was right there The gang's leader, a lanky man called Teegle, hammered the door with his fist and called, cheerfully, 'Comin' through.'

The friendly voice must have fooled the people behind the door, which was opened by one man, another one peering curiously over his shoulder.

The first man had a gun in his fist but it wasn't lifted.

Teegle got out of the way and the biggest member of the gang, Bronc, charged the door, knocking the guard sprawling, his iron falling, skittering along the floor behind him.

By then all the boys had their guns out.

The Miner, who'd dropped his gear on the floor, was menacing the passengers with a big old Dragoon Colt. He was bristle-faced and wild looking and the iron waving in his fist looked like a miniature cannon.

The first guard sat on his ass, blinking owlishly upwards.

The second man, his shotgun against the wall yards from him, had his hands high in the air.

They hadn't been very smart, these two.

Anyway, paid employees, why should they face down a battery of hardware in the hands of a bunch of hardcases with fire in their eyes?

Teegle made for the strongbox in the corner. He had an 'inside man' on the railroad and paid him well for information.

Bronc took the Miner's place. The older man shambled through the door, dragging his gear, joined Teegle, said:

'I'll fix this easy. Then we've got to get out of 'ere till she blows.'

The prisoners' hands were tied behind their backs. They were dragged out into the carriage. The boys followed them, the old powder-man bringing up the rear, shutting the door behind him. He had already put a lucifer to the trail of powder he'd made.

The train, on the flat again, had begun to pick up speed once more.

But it came to a sudden jarring halt as the driver caught sight of the pile of logs that had been piled on the steel rails ahead of him.

In the carriages passengers were flung about and there were yells and screams. But the hold-up men had known what was going to happen and braced themselves, expecting too the explosion that followed, this right behind them, shocking their ears.

Passengers were demoralized. But the two men in the small front cab heard the shattering,

11

echoing sound and the driver said, 'What in hell's that?'

His mate reached a pistol from his toolbox and said, 'We'll go see. Get your shotgun.'

The explosion had shaken the carriage. Amid the echoes a woman was screaming shrilly. Timber crashed. Dust and debris fell. But it seemed there wasn't any enormous damage. And nobody seemed to be hurt.

As the smoke was clearing, Teegle followed the Miner, who left his gear on the floor, carried gunny sacks instead. When the two men came back out those sacks were bulging.

The Miner was the first to the ground, suddenly agile, cock-a-hoop. Bronc had taken the sacks from him, and the older man swung his gear like a boy playing hookey, putting a spare finger or two to his mouth and making a shrill whistle, lingering with it.

The horses didn't have far to come and, used to this kind of signal, came at a gallop.

Everything had gone off like it was charmed. They hadn't even had to shoot anybody.

Mounted up, the gang got going, the Miner now in the rear after loading his stuff on his cayuse. Then the unforeseen happened.

From back in the train a gun sounded.

The Miner gave a small, choked cry and pitched from the saddle, dragging his stuff. Big

Bronc turned his horse about, took one look at the blood pouring from the oldster's head, jerked on the reins, turned about again, followed his friends.

The Miner didn't now have any of the *dinero* anyway.

And now more guns were going off back at the train. One of them mighty loud, a long weapon with two big muzzles by the sound of it. Something plucked at the top of Bronc's Stetson. He grabbed it and went low in the saddle.

TWO

Dan Dallobar stood somewhat awkwardly before the huge old desk and said, 'I was asleep, Cap'n. I was in a carriage sorta back, sorta next to where the thing happened but didn't have a blind notion about nothin' till the explosion woke me up.'

'For Pete's sake, sit down, Dan,' said Captain Marmaduke Rayson. 'You're giving me a headache looking up at you. And take that wide-awake off. Where in hell did you get a hat like that anyway?'

'In San Antone.' Dallobar drew up a wooden chair, sat down, doffed his big hat and hung it on one of his bony knees.

He looked across at the man behind the desk who, with side-whiskers and carefully brushed greying hair, looked like the English aristocrat he was supposed to have been. Arrogant cutting-edge voice too, if needs be, though he could've

14

picked that up in a bordello in New Orleans where some Southern bucks sort of talked that way.

Dallobar told himself that he didn't half-believe anything unless he had cast-iron proof.

He kind of liked the chief, though.

And the chief said, friendly-like, and with a thin smile on his jib, 'So you were on leave and you got drunk and you went to sleep on a train, not expecting any fuss whatever.'

'That's about the size of it, Cap'n. It was me who got that feller, though. The driver an' his fireman didn't start till after an' didn't hit a thing. I guess the gang was outa range by then – I dunno. I will admit my head was kind of fogged.'

'You hit something anyway.'

'Yeh. Is that fella dead?'

'Looked as if he was at first. Groove in the top of his head as if he'd been hit with an axe. Blood all over him.'

'What'll happen to him?'

'Quick trial. Then the pen. Hospitalized of course. His own cell, likely.'

Dallobar said, 'Yeh? An' that gives me an idea. I purely want that bunch, I surely do. I want 'em!'

Abel Teegle visited his railroad-informant acquaintance and was surprised to learn that the Miner was still alive. He hadn't known the old man at all well. But he had to admit that the oldster had done his job well and had decided he'd use him again if his particular talents were needed. But things happen – and Teegle had written the old cuss off.

Dead, he wouldn't be able to talk. And his share of the loot, though it would have been the lowest of the lot, could be split among the rest of the gang, a measure for the chief-o also.

Not that the haul had been anywhere near what had been expected. Teegle's weedy, shifty-eyed informant had told him that the bank money had to be the biggest that that line had handled. But that hadn't been the fact after all and Teegle was understandably peeved about it – and then some!

Hell, there'd only been two guards, and they hadn't been in any great shape. If there'd been porters, or maybe other guard personnel, the boys hadn't seen hide nor hair of 'em. Unless it was somebody like that who'd brought the Miner down.

Shifty-eyes had to take less *dinero* than he'd expected. Teegle figured he wouldn't use the man again, a braggart and a liar.

I ought to shoot the bastard, he reflected. But that might only cause more complications.

Maybe some sort of an 'accident' could be arranged at a later date.

Teegle's *segundo*, Rafe Poloi, would be able to handle that. Rafe never took chances, often chided his boss for being too reckless. He had been surprised that the train job had gone off without a hitch. But he was of course as peeved as the rest of them at the haul being a lot smaller than they'd expected.

As for big Bronc and the fourth member of the quartet, young Rip Colen, they were as reckless as their chief. They liked the fun, the noise. The killings maybe. They accepted their dues and that was it.

Teegle gave the crooked railroad-man a hard look, raised his finger to his lips, said, 'Easy. *Easy.*'

'Sure, Abe. Sure.' A rabbit. But was he as scared as he seemed to be? He had made amends, had gotten more information, told Teegle where the wounded Miner was being held in custody.

Back at the hideout Teegle passed this information to his boys.

'The Miner knows us all now an' he might talk ...'

'You're right, Abe,' put in Rafe Poloi. Bronc and Rip just nodded their heads and grinned.

'We've got to get 'im outa there,' Teegle said.

They had never worn masks, were known to the law, though not yet everywhere. They had reps among the owlhoot fraternity and that could be an asset. It was something Teegle was proud of and could use.

Their present hide out was a line hut which

had been disused and empty for years except when an old prospector used it for a while before disappearing into the unknown. Cattle and drovers didn't come this way. Spanish bayonet, cacti and tangled shrubbery spread over rocks and scrub grass. The wind swept across this wild, unwelcoming territory like a cluster of knives.

The hut was sheltered, though, partially hidden. A man could stand a little way from there and watch the surrounding territory for miles. Behind the hut there was a rise, tangled with vegetation, floored with shale. Anybody trying to come down there would be heard like a bunch of wildcats.

The boys never stayed there for long and there was always one or another of them out in the open on look-out.

'The leader was a man called Abel Teegle,' said Captain Marmaduke Rayson. 'Tall as you, Dan, but skinnier. Usually rides with a feller called Rafe Poloi. Nobody recognized the others on the train job.'

'Wisht I'd been awake,' complained Dan Dallobar, not for the first time.

'Forget it. We know that the old feller called the Miner was with the gang, might even have been hired for the first time to do what he did, the sort of thing he used to do underground. He might tell us things when he's able to. He's at a

18

doctor's in San Antonio. They can't give him a cell yet, but he's well guarded. What you suggested might work if we, and the captive, get that far. But I want you to try and get a line on the Teegle gang, see what can be done that end. Connections, huh, you've got 'em?'

'I have, chief,' said Dallobar with a twisted smile.

The older man watched the younger one go, moving like a lean cat, wished he could go along with him, riding the long trail.

The aftermath of wounds caught in the War Between the States prevented him from saddle-hopping.

Maybe I'll ride the trains, he thought, as he clambered slowly to his feet.

THREE

Teegle sent young Rip Colen in first. He wasn't
on any dodgers so far and was a personable looking young man with a sharp way who might well
be looking for a job as some sort of a guard or
maybe a look-out in a gambling set-up. San
Antone was a mighty open town since the war.

In truth, Rip already had some sort of ploy. He
left his mount at the livery stable after dismount-
ing, almost falling over as he did so, limping as he
regained his balance, saying with a painful
grimace, 'Damn cayuse threw me back on the
trail. Somep'n spooked 'im, dunno what, didn't
see a goddam thing, me.'

The old hostler was sympathetic. 'Twisted your
laig, huh?'

'Sort of my side, pain runs down my leg, feel I
oughta be in a damn' wheelchair or somep'n.' A
weak laugh, a painful twist of features, not
unhandsome, many a cathouse madam had told

Rip so; he'd once been a fancy bully-boy in a place.

'You ought to see a doctor.' That was just what Rip had wanted the old goat to suggest. Jerk of a gnarled thumb. 'One just down the street. You'll see the sign.'

'Thanks, friend.'

Rip limped away, made such a good job of it that he almost fell ass over brisket on the uneven sod.

He began to slow down, grimacing like a gargoyle but eyes watchful as he spotted the hard-looking character on the stoop of the surgery with the bright sign above it and well-scrubbed steps up to the door.

This is it, he thought, and without hesitation turned, limped across the street.

A couple of narrow steps led up to the stoop. Rip climbed them as if on a rocky trail to perdition. Then the gent on look-out said:

'The doc's not available today, son. Go up the alley a fair piece on. His locum's there. He'll see you han'some.'

The deep voice was affable, but the eyes above the rat-trap mouth and the hooked nose were flintlike.

Rip said 'Thanks' politely. Without too much difficulty, but limping all the time, he found the alley, turned into it. Then he quit his gammy act, hastened his steps, going right past the small surgery with the peeling sign on the door.

He went in through the side door of what appeared to be a cantina, and was; and he had a steaming *taco* and a couple of shots of tequila with the lemon-slice and the salt.

He listened to gossip from the various folk in the darkish place but didn't pick up anything of interest. He figured he had already filched the information he'd come to San Antone to get anyway, and he limped back to the livery stable.

The old hostler said, 'You don't seem so bad now ...' obviously aiming to go on, ask about the doc probably. Rip cut him short:

'Yeh, but I'll lead the nag for a bit first off, 'fore I test my riding.'

'Best thing,' the old man said.

Rip paid him good and bade him farewell, didn't mount the cayuse until they were well out of town.

Then he rode hard till Bronc, on look-out, waved to him. He dismounted, led the horse over the rough ground and greeted Teegle and Rafe Poloi.

'You done good, boy,' Teegle said. 'It'll be dark soon an' we'll see what *we* can do.'

Teegle rode with Rip by his side, the other boys way behind them in the main street of San Antone, the bright lights all around colouring the darkness. They were taking chances, even split

up as they were. But not even Rafe was grum-
bling overmuch any more.

They'd approached the town on the opposite
side from the way Rip had come in earlier, so they
hadn't had to pass the stables where the younker
had pulled his half-crippled act.

Rip indicated the place they were making for.
But he was puzzled also. It was quiet outside the
front of the surgery, didn't seem to be anybody
standing watch.

'Go round the back and check,' Teegle told him.
'I'll hold the boys, pretend I'd just met 'em.'

Nobody was around. Nobody was watching Rip.
There was an alley, Hell, like most Western
towns, built piece on piece, higgledy-piggledy, the
place was full of alleys, short cuts, strange nooks
and crannies.

Rip left his horse just inside the alley, went up
there soft-footed, didn't see a soul.

There was nobody outside the back of the doc's
place. A downstairs light shone in a window.
There hadn't been any light out front at all, Rip
reflected. Not in a window anyway, a proper light.
Only a small, sputtering jet to illuminate the
sign.

Leading his horse, the young man returned to
his chief who reined forward away from Rafe and
Bronc who were still pretending they didn't know
each other, though there was nobody around to be
bothered one way or another.

23

'Backaways,' said Teegle, leading, again the big ape and his companion bringing up the rear, a wide space between them.

Sort of lackadaisically, they all hitched their mounts onto a rack outside some kind of rathskeller. Teegle had talked out of the corner of his mouth at Rip who'd relayed his words to the other two. Teegle turned back the way they'd come. Just a short way. Bronc and his scurrying sidekick followed at discreet short intervals. Rip, pulling a peevish face, stayed near the horses.

Next to the establishment where a piano had just started up was a shop with women's fineries in the dimly lit window. It was as if this young man was waiting for some frail who was tardy, as frails tended to be.

Rip had lit up. He smoked a Mexican weed, scraped his high heel impatiently in the dust. But he was actually watching the quiet surgery all the while, and he had eyes like a wild lynx.

The back door was locked. While the other two stayed on look-out, stocky Rafe Poloi got to work with his knife. Soon he hissed 'All right', and eased the door gently open.

They filed into a tidy kitchen, obviously the back of the medico's private quarters, quiet, empty.

But then an old man came through a door opposite them; he must have heard something,

24

maybe had been awakened from a nap. His thin grey hair was awry, his eyes blinking. He took pince-nez from a rumpled shirt pocket, put them on, and stared at the three visitors.

He didn't look at all scared, even when each visitor showed him a gun.

He said, 'What do you boys want? You all look healthy enough.'

'We've got no time to waste, suh,' said Teegle. 'If you yell we'll fill you full of lead. Where's the prisoners, the wounded oldster?'

The doc gave a little cackle, then said, 'I figured you might be friends of his. You're too late, boys. He's not here. He was taken down to the jailhouse about half an hour ago and I was getting myself a little rest after my exertions. But the man will live I think. The law seems to think so anyway, though they took him away on a stretcher. I have more worthy patients to look after.'

The old man, who didn't want to get himself slugged, gave them no argument when they tied him up and gagged him. They laid him down on a rush mat. Poloi managed to lock the door after them. They returned to the waiting Rip who said he hadn't seen a thing.

Cap'n Rayson slid the two Wanted notices across the desk to Dan Dallobar, who was making his last visit before hitting the trail with provisions, a full belly, and plenty of water in his canteens.

'Messenger just brought them in. Dodgers on Abel Teegle and Rafe Poloi. It's reckoned they're still together.'

Dallobar took them, pocketed them. But then he got a surprise.

'I'm coming with you, Dan. We'll take the train. You can put your horse in the caboose. He's travelled like that before, hasn't he?'

'Oh, sure.'

Dallobar knew it wasn't any use arguing with the captain who was implacable, and sometimes cantankerous with it if his judgement was questioned.

Anyway, the big feller not only owed a great loyalty to the captain, he also liked him quite a lot.

He didn't watch as Rayson came lopsidedly around the desk and limped across the floor.

Dan Dallobar opened the door, held it wide, smiling.

'Let's go then, pardner,' he said.

FOUR

It had been a busy day at the livery stables. The kid who helped out had been laid up with croup and had only just returned to his tasks, making up for lost time. The old hostler was having a well-earned lie-down in his den, and, working under lantern light, the kid was cleaning up.

He had raised a lot of dust and his head was beginning to grow a sickening ache. Skittish horses didn't help at all. There was still a bunch of them left. The town was booming.

There was an elderly bad-tempered dun-coloured mare that a half-drunk mossyhorn had left for a while. She had already sneakily tried to kick the hostler's boy and he was wary of her. But he was overtaken by a spasm of coughing, shaking as if in a sudden wind, staggering him sweating under the dust, under the yellow lights.

He got too near the mare and she lashed sneakily backwards, and got the kid in the knee.

He went down, squealing for his boss who, bleary-eyed, came rushing in.

The boy's knee was already swelling like a balloon.

'We gotta get you to the doc,' the old man said.

He helped the boy along. If he remembered the other limping younker he had already seen that day, the well-set-up one who had been tossed from his horse, he did not mention the fact.

They went up the front steps of the surgery, discovered that the door wasn't locked and stepped into darkness. But a light glimmered from the back.

'Doc,' the hostler called.

They heard a thumping, then a muffled cry. They went through to the kitchen.

The doc had had a set of false teeth made expertly by a dentist friend of his. He had managed to chew his gag and spit it out, and had crawled to a cupboard so that he could bang his feet, slippered though they were, against the rattling door.

While the hostler let him free, the doc was talking all the time, concluding, 'I'll look after the boy. You go and give the alarm.'

The hostler went back out the front, down the street, hoping he wasn't too late, that gunfire wouldn't erupt suddenly in front of him.

The boys had moved the horses and found a place for them around the back of town, a stand of spindly trees of indeterminate species behind a disused, leaning privy that looked like an upended coffin threatening to fall to dust.

Rip, still somewhat peeved, was to be the horse-handler. Hell, he said, if it wasn't for him the boys wouldn't have known where to go, what to do.

Teegle, high-falutin' again suddenly, told him not to exaggerate. 'You might have to cover our retreat,' he added.

Were they gonna kill the Miner or just bring him out, Rip wondered. He didn't ask, just acted mollified and waited while Teegle, Poloi and Bronc dissolved in the night. A sliver of moon glimmered. Out here it was silent as a graveyard.

The old hostler, whose name was Dick, ran into a young deputy called Tubs who was portly but faster than he looked. Tubs had a spare gun and he handed this to Dick who had insisted that he'd follow through all the way, no matter what happened. No goddam owlhooters were gonna hurraw his town! Besides, the doc was an old friend of his.

Dick said he'd toted a badge himself in days gone by. Tubs believed the feisty old-timer who acted now as if he was about to enjoy himself.

Rafe Poloi had come round from the back to make sure the jail was where they'd figured it would be.

He didn't spot Dick and Tubs and, if he had, would have taken them for passers-by. Tubs wasn't wearing his badge, seldom did around town. The genial, plump boy was well known and, as lawmen go, well liked.

There were plenty of passers-by now at this time of night. Rafe was one of them also till he returned to his friends, jerked a thumb and hissed, 'Back door.'

There was no guard but, understandably, the door was locked. Rafe Poloi worked with his knife and the door swung open. The three men eeled through, Teegle in the lead now.

Guns were ready. There was just a passage. The cells weren't in sight. There was another closed door straight ahead.

This was not locked. Teegle lifted the latch, eased the wood a tiny bit without a creak.

He opened it wide with sudden force and went through, the other two flanking him on either side then; not the first time they'd used this ploy and seen it pay off in more ways than a few.

They were confronted by two men, one elderly, the other young, quicker, reaching for a gun on the edge of the desk behind which the other man had risen.

'Hold it, bucko,' Teegle barked.

Faced by the killing menace of three levelled shooters, the young man froze, lifted his clawed hand away from the weapon on the desk.

'Get your hands up, both o' you,' Teegle told them, and they complied.

Five men under the yellow lamplight. Three guns ready, lethal.

But everybody was taken by surprise at the opening of the door from the street and the plump deputy and, behind him, the old hostler, came through. Tubs was a lot faster than he looked. He drew, levelled, thumbed a hammer. Rafe Poloi took the slug full in the chest and it drove him backwards as if by a blow from a giant hammer.

The deputy by the desk was already reaching for the gun again. This time he got it. But he also got a pill from Abe Teegle's weapon and spun, staggering into his friend Tubs, preventing the plump deputy from firing again and getting in the way of Dick who had also pulled his pistol.

The older man behind the desk had pulled a gun from the drawer by his waist, but the deputies were staggering into the line of fire: the one with a shattered shoulder, and Tubs, who was striving to bring his gun level again.

'Out!' shouted Abe Teegle, and Bronc and he backed.

Hostler Dick fired a shot at the retreating pair, missed Bronc's big head by a whisker. Then the two men were through the middle door, slamming it, leaving the blue smoke and the stink of cordite behind them.

They got through the back and ran, both of them luckily unhurt. They reached Rip Colen and the horses.

'I heard shootin'. Where's Rafe?'

'He's dead. We've got to get out of here.'

There was pursuit but it was some way back and shots winged after them with no success as they rode. Rafe Poloi's riderless horse tagged along, forging ahead, then coming back, tossing his head as if to say 'What in hell's the matter with you slow coaches?; he seemed to be hugely enjoying himself.

The Miner was scared. He thought a mob had busted into the jail with the intention of lynching him.

He was told, hell, he wasn't that important.

He learned that in fact the dangerous visitors had been friends of his aiming to let him free.

Or maybe just aiming to do him for good, shut his mouth.

One of them, identified as Rafe Poloi, had been shot stone dead.

The Miner said he didn't know anybody of that name. But the folks didn't seem to believe him. He was left in his billet. Right now none of the other cells seemed to be occupied.

The Miner lay back. His mind was in turmoil. He didn't feel at all good.

FIVE

Dallobar and the captain had travelled by night and the lanky young feller, a horseman who didn't much like iron horses that puffed irritably, hadn't been able to sleep too good.

It was early morning when the two travellers reached San Antonio. Marmaduke Rayson had sent messages ahead and when Dallobar and he got to town three more operatives were there to meet them in a secret place, just a disused barn.

They split up again, though, after the captain had confabbed with them. Only Rayson and Dallobar stayed together; they went to a cantina. Then the three other men turned up again, pretending they didn't know each other, or the tall man and his elderly companion, who looked like a cross between a card-sharp and an Eastern cattle-buyer who at one time had fallen off a horse, the way he limped an' all.

The place began to fill up. The captain disappeared for a while. Dallobar, sitting alone, listened with interest to talk of an attempted jail-bust, a feller called Rafe Poloi being killed, a deputy wounded.

It was getting towards noon and the place was full of folks of all stripes and nationalities; a regular rabble, and a babble to make your head spin.

Marmaduke Raynor returned, sat on his own, pulled his ear a few times as if it itched. Dallobar got the signal and got himself set.

The other three operatives were mingling, still not eyeing each other but coming a mite closer, it seemed.

They usually worked together, Dallobar remembered, two of 'em anyway. One playing the hard bucko, the other the understanding one, changing places sometimes of course, both affable characters by nature but mighty good at their job.

They had good records of putting miscreants in jail, shooting a few.

Dallobar didn't think he'd seen the third man before. Right now all three of them behaved like cowhands on a spree.

Dallobar knew that the captain always worked within the laws of the land, wouldn't have it any other way, and speedily dismissed any operative who stepped out of line.

Up to a point anyway....

How he loved that title 'operative'! Maybe the

law kind of liked it too. Older lawmen in particular respected the chief and his organization and, in the main, co-operated with his folk.

Dallobar had been with the organization a pretty fair while after a chequered career in other fields.

He had heard with no displeasure that, in a weak moment maybe, the chief had referred to Dan Dallobar as his 'prime troubleshooter'.

Well, Dallobar reflected, I ain't had the education many of the other boys have had, but I sure as hell have had the experience of the seamier side of the wild South-western territories.

Two of the three men Dallobar was watching were now coming together. Just now he couldn't see the third man. But the two others met; they seemed to bump. One of them shouted, the words blanketed by the general din of the saloon but obviously not complimentary.

One man seemed to be reaching for a gun. The other hit him with a roundhouse swing to his jib, sending him staggering into a third operative who had reappeared in Dallobar's sight; he had moved in quickly but, purely by chance, it seemed, had gotten in the way.

The third man staggered and cannoned into a fourth man who wasn't part of the ploy at all, just happened to be conveniently placed, becoming an asset to what had been planned by the initial protagonists.

And now Dallobar was rising, after a quick glance at the captain who was still sitting like a wooden Indian outside a cathouse.

Other folks were a-moving and a-jostling.

Folks with pugnacious merriment in their eyes. Others with malice; definitely.

Somebody yelled 'Fight!' – this in jubilation.

Dallobar waded in. Suddenly bodies surrounded him on all sides.

Somebody clipped him on the ear, bending him, making his head sing. He swung around, shoved his fist into a grinning hatchet-face with a handsome handlebar moustache.

The face disappeared, moustache and all. A small man kicked Dallobar indignantly in the kneecap. The lanky operative said 'Ouch' and crumpled a little. But he managed to take the diminutive attacker under his armpit and sling him at an approaching big feller. The two became entangled in a knee-tying heap. Dallobar ploughed on, limping a little, but his head clearing.

He caught sight of two of the quarrelsome trio who had engineered this mêlée. He surged forward to help them. He couldn't see the third operative. A fancy-looking young gent came at him swinging a bottle. He ducked and felt the wind across the top of his scalp. He had left his big hat back on his seat, hadn't wanted to maybe lose it in the mêlée. He raised his knee and his assailant gulped and crumpled, his improvised weapon smashing to the floor.

Suddenly Dallobar was in the grip of a man who was taller than he was and certainly heavier and had a hug like an irate grizzly. Knees were no good here. And the lean feller's arms were pinned to his side.

He used his head, butting, then raking upwards, an old street-fighter's ploy. The giant went 'Ug!', his head jerking back, his bear like grip slackening. Blood spurted from his nose and Dallobar managed to rase his left hand, balled into a fist. He used it like a club and the giant was half-driven down, half-driven backwards. Dallobar knew he had to finish him; went after him, both hands free now and he using them as pounding fists driving the giant to his knees and then flooring him completely, folks tumbling over him.

And then Dallobar caught sight of the third operative. The one he didn't know too well. He was on his knees as if he were praying, blood dripping from his chin and splattering the floor.

Dallobar surged forward, bent over the man. But then he was hit very hard on the back of the head.

He plunged into a sort of fog which covered him completely.

SIX

He was sitting on his butt without nobody paying him mind. He was conscious by then but owl-eyed. The law picked him up and, when he came completely to his senses, he was sitting in a cell. A nervous-looking elderly gent was sitting opposite him. There was nobody else in this billet they shared.

The Miner?

Probably.

'Where's my hat?' Dallobar wanted to know.

The other man said, 'I ain't seen no hat.'

Then, however, there was a lot of noise from the cell next door.

Didn't need any great figuring to determine that that barred accommodation was now occupied by Dallobar's three fellow operatives, courtesy Marmaduke Rayson and the local star packers.

Weapons were of course missing. Dallobar sat on his bunk and raised his hand to the back of his head and felt the duck-egg there. No skin broken, good thing.

The din was still going on next door. Dallobar raised his head, wincing, threw it back, yowled like an inebriated coyote.

His elderly cell-mate looked more nervous than ever.

Dallobar was still noisily bemoaning the loss of his hat.

A voice seemed to be answering from the front office, with more words obviously irate but unintelligible to the men in the cells; though somebody next door to the lean feller and his elderly cell-mate – and it was comparatively quiet now next-door – complained that he was getting a headache.

Then the communicating door between the cell-block and the front of the jail was opened and a man strode through.

He was stocky, powerful-looking, middle aged, with a bald top but lush, greying sideburns that reached down nearly to his jawbones. He wore a furious expression on a broad clean-shaven face. He carried no gunbelt or keys but something was crumpled largely in one big hand. Looked like a hat.

It was a hat and it was screwed up smaller and shoved through the bars of the cell.

'Here's your fancy headgear. Now will you quit your caterwauling?'

'You'll ruin it,' complained Dallobar, charging forward. He grabbed the hat and pulled it through.

'Where in Hades did you get a hat like that?' demanded the heavy-set, middle aged individual who had a silver star on his breast which matched his bright, irate eyes.

'I'm sick o' folks asking me that,' said Dallobar, sitting back on his bunk and straightening out the headgear. It could have been a Mexican sombrero. But it wasn't quite that, though the brim was wide and curved. The top, though, wasn't what could be called steeple-like, and it had cute dimples which its owner now stroked and pressed with affection; then he straightened out the ornate band, wide, garish, snakelike.

The door slammed behind the heavy-set lawman and all was quiet.

'That got rid of him then, didn't it, ol' socks?' the tall prisoner said to his elderly companion.

'Sure did.' Spoken without much conviction, though, it seemed.

'I guess you're the train-robber I was told about, huh?'

The older man nodded his grey head but avoided the tough, lanky man's eyes. He was reminded of Abe Teegle, another lanky man, a desperate man as this one also seemed to be. Not

the kind of character that anybody would choose
to be locked up with. Not the way the Miner was
beginning to figure things now. He wished he'd
never set eyes on Teegle.... But the other tall
feller was going on:

'I heard that your pards tried to get you outa
here an' a deputy got shot.'

'He ain't daid,' said the Miner weakly.

'I was a bank robber once,' the lean, rough-
looking character said brightly.

'Do tell,' said the Miner, then wished he hadn't.

'Hell, I was just a baby,' the character said.

The Dallobars had a small ranch and ran it
themselves: man, wife, one young son. But the
man was a gambler and often neglected his
duties. Then he was shot to death – a stray bullet
in a saloon brawl – and his wife and son strug-
gled along.

Then the woman – not a good judge of the male
gender – married a drummer who happened
along selling feminine knick-knacks. He turned
out to be a charmer with some very nasty streaks
in his nature. He didn't much like ranching,
vented his spleen on the woman and the boy,
driving the latter to work at even the hardest of
chores.

The woman became ailing. The boy worked
while his stepfather caroused with cronies in the
nearby town; he became a sort of a go-between for

the hard-hats who preyed on the decent folk.

The boy grew bigger and one day he stepped between the two adults, fearful that the man would finally kill the sick woman.

The woman ran to the barn, half demented, screaming. The man floored the boy, chased the woman. The boy scrambled to his feet and followed. In the barn the man had a whip; he turned on the boy with it. The boy, strong in his fury, grabbed the whip and struck out. The man, cut across the neck, staggered, fell, and hit his head on a steel bucket, one of the battered articles which littered the dirt floor of the gloomy place.

The mother told her son to run, but he wouldn't. Then it was too late – they heard hoofbeats. Some of the fallen man's cronies had called for him.

Some of them held the woman, didn't treat her right – at all. Others took the boy outside and started to string him up from a crosspiece outside the barn.

But the Fates took a hand then – in the guise of more riders led by the woman's brother who called from time to time; more than ever recently, worried for his kin, wanting to get the woman and the boy away from there. Not a smart man, though, this brother. An owlhooter with grandiose ideas but not much to back them up with.

42

He and his boys were a match for the other
bunch, however, who fled, carrying two wounded
with them, and also the man from the barn, the
husband, slung over the front of the saddle of a
horse ridden by the youngest member of the
tribe, the one who had looked up to the brutal ex-
drummer the most.

Young Dan Dallobar was saved.

The brother and his men had a job planned.
They left his sister with a friend at a smallholding on their journey's way.

Young Dan held the horses while the others hit
a bank, hoping for a big payroll. But they'd got
their day wrong. All they did was scare an old
caretaker half to death.

Relenting later, the leader left his nephew with
an old friend whom he'd served with during the
war: his old captain, Marmaduke Rayson.
Marmaduke was a man who had friends in many
places, high and low.

He discovered that young Dan's stepfather was
not dead as had first been thought. He'd gotten
well and had disappeared. Nobody seemed to
know where he was now. Anyway, Dan wasn't
wanted for anything. He visited his Ma who was
still at the smallholding where she'd been taken
on that fateful day.

Sick and worn out, she died in her son's arms.
The boy went looking for the man he blamed for
her death. While he searched he matured,

became hard the way he figured he'd have to be.

He found a grave, heard a story of a man who had badly treated another woman and had been shot to death by the woman's brother, who was free now – Dan shook his hand, hadn't seen him since.

But that seemed such a long time ago....

He hadn't really told the Miner much. Hadn't thought the old goat was listening much anyway, wasn't sure that he'd been talking all that much himself, not really, things running through his mind all the time.

Some things he wanted to forget. Most of 'em.... But they'd done plenty of things together, him and the chief, since those early days, since the inception of the Range Investigation Agency. And with operatives like those who now languished in the cell next door.

Right now the Miner was more or less awake, staring at his young cell-mate – who certainly didn't seem as drunk as he had before.

'We'll get you out of here, old-timer, me an' my pards,' this character said. 'Then I want to meet your ol' friend, what's-his-name? Teegle, that's it, ain't it? He sounds like a character that him an' me can do some profitable things together, huh? Huh?'

SEVEN

They were back in the line hut where they'd been before. Abe Teegle was in a foul mood. Nothing seemed to have gone as well lately as it used to do. And now Rafe Poloi was gone for good, and Rafe had been Abe's long-time *segundo*.

Big Bronc had never been a talkative cuss. And young Rip Colen was quiet because he had been bitten by something. Maybe on the ride. Or maybe even here in the hut where he had rest-lessly slept, saying they should've kept riding – and Teegle telling him to shut his pesky gab.

Rip didn't talk much after that. But he started to moan, clutching his leg. Bronc rolled his pants down for him, to discover the boy's thigh was red and painfully swollen.

He wouldn't be able to ride even if they started out now in the very early, misty morning.

'Look after him,' Teegle said. 'I'll go on. I have to stash this loot. I'll get in touch.'

45

Bronc was stupid. But he wasn't *that* stupid! He followed Teegle outside.

'We oughta share out now,' he said.

Teegle was ahead. He turned. He had his gun in his hand. Bronc of course hadn't had an inkling that the man had drawn it. And Bronc did a foolish thing. He reached downwards. And Teegle shot him in the belly.

The force of the slug at such close quarters drove Bronc backwards, his big hands away from his gun and clawing at his middle.

He fell forward on his face.

Teegle reached his horse, mounted up. He didn't give the hulk in the dust another look but began to urge his mount forward, the precious loot already slung. But then he stopped the beast.

One shot had been fired. A few more wouldn't make such difference now. Down from his horse, Teegle unhitched Rip's and Bronc's cayuses and the spare one that had belonged to Rafe Poloi. He fired shots into the air and shrieked, setting them off at a frantic gallop, raising the dust.

Teegle rode his own mount in a different direction.

The Miner had been awake quite a while and dawn had broken. He didn't have the white bandage on his head now and the local doc had said he was going to be all right. If he didn't eventually get his neck stretched, that was.

However the elderly ex-train bandit (what a useless hoot that had been!) still had a man-sized headache and started when his cell-mate said:

'Just stay quiet, ol' hoss.'

Then the lean man sat up in his bunk, threw his head back and yowled like a crazy coyote.

It was Deputy Tubs who came into the cell-block, not carrying a weapon, just a plump, red and furious face.

The noisy prisoner quietened, just laughed, rose, loped over to the bars. Then he did a sort of contortion and pulled a gun from someplace around one of his boots.

To the startled Miner it hardly looked like a gun at first. But then he recognized it as a single-barrelled derringer which, despite its toylike aspect, could blow a hole right through a man at such close range.

Tubs recognized it too all right, backing a little till the lanky man snapped:

'That's far enough.'

Tubs halted, his hands half raised.

'Call the other one, my friend,' the man with the pistol said. 'Tell him to bring the keys. If I see a gun anyplace near him I'll blow you to Kingdom Come.'

Tubs licked his lips, half-turned his head, yelled, 'Sharper! Bring the keys in here, please, will you? No guns or there'll be hell to pay. You hear me?'

47

'I hear you.' The voice was fainter, but clear.

The middle-aged lawman with the formidable bearing and the formidable sideburns came through. He was bare of hardware except the gleaming, businesslike bunch of keys.

'Give 'em to him.' The prisoner jerked his head in the direction of Tubs, the deadly little weapon in his fist not wavering even a fraction.

Sharper handed the keys over and Tubs unlocked the cell-door. Then the prisoner jerked his little gun and ordered, 'Let the other boys out.' He stepped out himself, with his free hand waving the Miner forward while Tubs unlocked the other door and his older sidekick stood like a graven image, but obviously a mighty furious one.

The boys next door had been strangely quiet but now they all filed out grinning like happy cats.

'Better tie these two cookies up,' said the lean prisoner with the little gun.

One of the other men went through the middle door, then soon returned with a coil of rawhide.

The two lawmen were bound, then gagged with their own kerchief, Tubs quiet, Sharper cussing like a drunken muleskinner till his mouth was stopped.

All the members of the bunch found their guns in the office, except for the Miner who searched for his faithful Dragoon without success. Nobody offered to lend him a weapon.

'Stay by me,' the one called Dan said.

They all seemed to be able to find horses all right. There were more out in the streets this early morning than the Miner had expected to see. These boys were daring, unconventional. The Miner had never heard of a jailbreak being pulled by daylight before, and without a shot being fired either. No darkness, just a morning mist and a pale sun shining through.

Marmaduke Rayson went through the back door of the jailhouse which had been left conveniently unlocked. He went into the cell-block and picked up the bunch of keys that had been tossed, as if carelessly, on the floor. He unlocked the door behind which the two lawmen lay on a bunk apiece like a couple of trussed turkeys awaiting Thanksgiving.

He ungagged and untied his old friend Sharper and young Tubs.

'It took you long enough,' Sharper said. 'Why didn't your boys leave the gags off so we could've shouted?'

'You might have fetched somebody too soon.'

'Yeh, I suppose you're right.' Sharper groaned, stretching his big body. 'I hope to hellfire that this thing works out like you planned.'

'It was Dan Dallobar's idea in the first place.'

'He played it well, I'll say that for him.'

'So did you it seems, old friend.'

'It was a good job Solly wasn't here,' Tubs said, 'he's kinda cantankerous.'

Solly was the other deputy, the one who'd got himself pinked during the Abe Teegle attack on the hoosegow.

The would-be jail-buster, Rafe Poloi, was lying in the ice-house waiting to be hidden under the sod.

'I'm kinda cantankerous myself,' said Sharper. 'With the boys millin' around an' Solly goin' off half-cocked I didn't even get me one shot at that bastard Teegle.'

'Your day will come,' said Marmaduke Rayson, somewhat cryptically.

EIGHT

Rip Colen was suffering. The pain, the delirium, the sleeping, the nightmarish awakening were all part of the suffering; and he didn't know what was real and what was nightmare.

He had thought he heard shooting. It was as if he was in a battle. Was that part of a delirium?

He had had a dream, though. He remembered the dream.

There was a cupboard against the opposite wall of the cabin, the wall opposite to where he lay, that backed on to the rising ground and bushes, tangled creepers and tufted hillocks.

Teegle used the bunk against the wall at the left of Rip. Bronc had a pallet on the floor and a bearskin next to the narrow door which was stout, however, and kept out the draughts. Rafe Poloi, who hadn't been any bigger then Rip, had slept in a corner swathed in blankets, like a squaw with a belly-ache. But Rafe would never be here or anyplace any more, belly-ache or no.

And Bronc preferred his pallet on the floor. He had once been a buffalo hunter, bragged about the enormous amount of the shaggy beasts he'd brought down.

The cupboard was against the back wall, the protected wall. While Bronc was outside tending the horses and Rip lay on his bed of sickness, Rip had seen Abe at the cupboard. But he hadn't opened the door, which was only full of provisions. He had instead used a lot of strength to swing the cupboard away from the wall.

And thus was revealed a cavity. And from this hiding place Abe had taken the gunny sacks that held the loot from the train robbery.

Rip hadn't seen the man put this boodle there in the first place.

But had he imagined all this? Had it been all part of a delirium?

How could he have made up something like that, something out of a kind of fairy tale?

The shots? Had the shots been all part of the same thing. But, still an' all, there were far more weapons than just guns and plenty of men – Bronc an' Teegle fr' instance – who could use any other weapon. A knife, a club, bare hands, boots. Bronc had huge hands. And large boots.

Rip thought he could hear himself laughing. He slipped in and out of consciousness....

But all of this ... were these things all dreams?

Or had his two pards gone, left him here to die?

It was so quiet out there....

'It's up ahead,' the Miner said. 'But I think that if we go any nearer on this side an' there's a look-out he'll spot us. That rise ahead – best we get around the back o' that. We want to go in easy don't we, don't want any mishaps?'

'Granted, ol' hoss,' said Dallobar. 'You lead the way. Carefully now, huh?'

There were just the two of them now. They hadn't seen anybody else in front or behind.

The older man made a detour, then halted in the shelter and cover of a tangle of underbrush which was however tall enough to cover him and his companion even if they stayed in the saddle.

The Miner pointed downwards to where they could see the roof of the line hut and past that the clearing.

Dallobar reached into his warbag and brought forth a small brass telescope.

'Won this at poker,' he said, and raised it to his eye. 'There's a man in the clearing, lying on the ground, still, as if he's dead. Take a look.'

He handed the glass to the Miner who at first seemed to have trouble focusing, swore, but then said, at last:

'It's Bronc, the big feller. He's mighty still all right. But what would he be doin' lyin' out there on his own? Seems to be somep'n funny goin' on.'

'We can tether the hosses, go down there.'

'Sure.'

The older man brought up the rear. The hut was quiet. The sun was hot on the back of their necks. They went round to the side. Dallobar shielded his eyes with his hand and peered through the dirt-smeared window, squinting.

He whispered, 'There's a man lyin' in a bunk, seems to be sleepin'. Can't see anybody else.'

They moved again.

The man in the bunk, identified by the Miner as Rip Colen, did not stir. The giant Bronc did not stir either; he was well and truly dead.

Dallobar and his companion didn't find any horses.

Rip's anguished eyes stared up into the lean man's hatchety but not unhandsome features.

Rip's pants were down around his ankles. The lean man said, 'I dunno what bit you, son, but the place is fillin' with pus an' I'll have to get that out.'

Rip made a croaking sound but also nodded his head slightly. The Miner came through the door carrying a stick from which he'd peeled the bark. He also had some clean cloths he'd taken from Dallobar's saddle-bag.

The stick was put in Rip's mouth and he bit hard on it with his strong white teeth. Dallobar took out his jack-knife, scratched a lucifer taken from a small box, and held the wicked-looking blade in the flame.

'This is gonna hurt some,' he said, bending over his patient.

Rip stiffened. The blade dug, probed. But quickly, neatly. Rip went 'Aaa-aah' and the stick was propelled from his lips and struck the Miner in the ear. But the job was done.

Rip passed out while Dallobar was doing the bandaging with torn strips of cloth after swabbing the wound with water from his canteen. There was no pump, no waterhole near, the Miner said. The boys had always had to make sure they had full canteens, same as the rannies who'd used this billet beforehand no doubt.

'Looks like Teegle left Rip here,' the Miner said. 'An' shot Bronc an' ran the hosses off.'

Rip, coming around later, was able to add more meat to the old-timer's conjecture. But not before he'd asked the powerful-looking, tall character to do something for him.

He pointed and said, 'Will you swing that cupboard away from the wall, *amigo*? It'll go with a big tug I think.'

It did, revealing the cavity behind.

'Hell, I thought I'd dreamed it,' Rip said. He lay back. 'I've got to think again.' He closed his eyes, obviously not right out of the woods yet.

Dallobar glanced back at the cupboard which

was still away from the wall the way he'd left it, the empty gap revealed behind.

He began to wonder whether Rip was playing possum. The colour had come back into the young man's face. He looked unhurt now, peaceful even. He was a healthy young cuss with fine powers of recovery.

Dallobar began to get impatient. He feigned anxiety, saying, 'You all right, son?'

Maybe Rip was fooled. He opened his eyes anyway.

Dallobar said, 'Your friend, Bronc, is dead in the dust not far from that open door.' He pointed a finger, almost accusingly, it seemed, though it wasn't actually aimed at the man in the bunk.

'I was too sick to investigate,' Rip said. 'I thought the shooting I'd thought I heard was part of a dream, all a dream.'

'All the hosses are gone,' said the Miner.

Rip spurted with laughter, shook, began to cough. Spluttering, he said, 'Looks like Teegle made a fool of us, huh, old-timer?'

'He had the loot anyway. Stashed it I guess.'

'Yeh, in that hole.'

The Miner was swearing wrathfully, colourfully. Dallobar cut in.

'I can't hang about.' He jerked a thumb at Rip who was sitting up now. 'You'll have to stay with him.'

'I want to come ...'

'Me too,' said Rip. 'I figure I can ride now.' He seemed to be changing his tune. The boodle was a big magnet.

'We haven't got another horse.'

Rip didn't seem to hear him. Eyes wide, furious. 'I want that sonabitch ... *Hell, he was makin' time with my sister.*'

NINE

Dallobar said, 'Rip's got to have a horse, yeh. I'll get him one. There's a smallholding we passed, not far back, I spotted with my spyglass. I reckon I ought to be able to get a mount there.'

The Miner said, 'What if there's a posse an' you're spotted?'

'If I figure I can't get back I'll fire three shots off. And you best get goin' if that happens. Don't worry about me. You'll have to ride two in the saddle, that's all.'

'We can do that,' said Rip, obviously now plumb raring to go.

But the Miner said, 'All right, pardner,' and sounded as if he meant it.

Dallobar had a plan, didn't know whether it would work or not, figured he'd have to try it anyway.

'Stay an' rest. Nobody's gonna bother you here.' He hoped that was the truth.

He went. He knew that two of the operatives, his companion jail-baiters, had been trailing him and the Miner at a discreet distance, something they were mighty good at, better than any law-posse Dallobar had ever seen.

They were surprised to see him. He talked fast, explaining why he badly needed a horse. One of them remonstrated, but the other, who knew Dallobar better, said:

'I've got some moccasins in my warbag. I don't mind walking a fair bit if I can get in the saddle occasionally.'

'All right,' said his partner. 'Give him your horse then.'

'You can turn back,' Dallobar said. 'I'll take things along from now on.'

'All right, Dan, what you say goes, the Cap'n explained that.'

'Yeh, so he did I guess.' Dallobar knew that Rayson and the other operative had stayed behind to join the posse led by Sharper and Tubs, who were following the plot through and going in a completely different direction from Dallobar himself and his jail-break associate, the Miner. The posse had to put on a show for the townsfolk, hadn't they? And Cap'n Rayson would stay at the big, low-lying adobe jailhouse, taking the place of his old friend Sharper for a while. Until the posse came back empty-handed anyway.

Dallobar had asked about Sharper, who had

taken his part so well during the break. As had Tubs also of course. The Cap'n had said the older lawman had been his sergeant in the Confederate army, had been the finest shot with a rifle that his then superior had ever seen, ever would see.

This wizard marksman had been dubbed 'Sharpshooter', later shortened to Sharper, and that moniker had followed him into civilian life. He hadn't seemed to mind, was maybe kind of proud of it, though he'd never say so of course.

Dallobar got back to the line hut with the spare horse. 'I got the whole gear as well,' he said.

They didn't ask him how, or whether he'd had to shoot anybody. He lied, told them he hadn't seen anything like a posse, which was partly true after all.

Rip said he'd been thinking and, although his thoughts hadn't been pleasant, he'd figured out – had an inkling anyway – where Abel Teegle might be.

'We've got to bury Bronc,' said the Miner.

Dallobar figured they could have done that, those two, while he was dickering for a spare horse for Rip. But he went along – and the dead giant's bulk was hidden under rocks where no predators could get at him.

Then they rode, Rip leading now, Dallobar keeping a close eye on him, not trusting him all the way at all. Rip was sharper than the Miner, who was treating Dallobar now like a bosom friend. Well, he'd got the oldster out of jail, hadn't he? But young Rip was a different mess o' fish altogether.

Seemed like Teegle had taken all the guns with him. But the Miner had two he had stolen back at the jail, where he'd been moaning that he couldn't find his old Dragoon Colt. He had given his spare gun to Rip and Dallobar couldn't make any objection to this without showing his hand in a funny way, which was the last thing he would've wanted to do.

Rip was pushing the pace.

Her name was Mercy. She went by her married name of Hipkiss. But Johnny Hipkiss was long gone. He'd gone to the gold fields to make a fortune for both of them, but he'd never returned, rich or poor. And Mercy had recently heard, from a distant neighbour who had come back impoverished from the dream Eldorado that had turned to dust, that Johnny had died from a fever up there and had had a miner's funeral.

Too far, Mercy had thought, *too far*. And now Johnny was a gentle memory and she was alone except for a neighbouring woman who visited from time to time. But she had a husband and two kids and a small ranch to run.

The woman said Mercy shouldn't be on her smallholding all alone. But Mercy's place was nearer to the small neighbouring town. She had friends there she could visit, and folks came out to buy her produce; vegetables, chickens, the pies and cakes she baked so well, her special frank-furters and even the succulent *tacos* her elderly Mexican friend, Josetta, had taught her to make.

But Josetta was gone now, a victim of fever, maybe the same kind of fever that had taken Johnny too in that far place.

Mercy was so busy that she did not pause to think what a sad life she had had, particularly more lately in her twenties. She was now twenty-nine and a shapely pretty-faced young woman with thick, rich, dark hair which she tied in a sort of pony-tail at the back of her head so that it didn't get in her way when she bent to her various tasks.

Both her parents had died suddenly in a stage-coach accident; the vehicle had plunged into a deep ravine and only the driver had been left alive to tell the tale, he having leapt free before the coach hit bottom and virtually exploded, killing the passengers and the shotgun guard.

Payroll money that the vehicle had carried, ensconced in a heavy brassbound chest, had been recovered unspoiled. At that time Mercy and Johnny had received a modicum of compensation, which hadn't lasted long, for Mercy's only surviving relative, her brother – called Rip for all time – had called and collected what he'd called his 'cut'.

Since then Rip had called at the smallholding but once, just after the news of Johnny's demise. At that time Rip had three companions: Abel Teegle, Rafe Poloi, and the big man they called Bronc.

The latter two hadn't had much to say, but the leader, Teegle, had been a soul of courtesy to the widowed girl. He had called later on his own and given her a gift of a silk scarf he said he'd picked up at the border, had thought of her as soon as he saw the prettily patterned thing.

She hadn't wanted to accept the gift at first, thinking that it wasn't the proper thing to welcome such from a man she'd known so briefly. But he had been insistent – had frightened her a little even though she was attracted to him also – and she had succumbed. He was a man who liked his own way.

Rip had called a few days later, also on his own, and had not seemed pleased to learn that his sister had accepted a gift from his friend, Abe. Such a small gift, Mercy had said, finding herself defending the other man now.

She had not seen either of them since.

Until that day at noontime when she thought the approaching horseman was a townie – she had a new batch of pies ready – but finally recognized Abe Teegle. She watched him dismount, opened the door to greet him.

He did not waste much time in preliminaries.

He said, 'I am a rich man now and I want you to come with me.'

When the trio came in sight of the smallholding, which lay in a shallow valley, the sun was going down redly behind it but was still bright. Dan Dallobar and Rip Colen raised their hands to shield their eyes. The Miner slumped in his saddle, half asleep it seemed.

'It's quiet down there,' Rip said. 'And I can't see any smoke coming from the chimneys. Mercy does a lot of cooking and baking. There was allus smoke coming from the chimneys.'

'The place looks deserted,' Dallobar said.

It was surrounded by neat vegetable gardens – he could see that now – and there were some flowers and shrubs, colourful splashes. Suddenly he thought he saw something moving. He squinted his eyes. Then he was startled as Rip said, 'There's somebody comin' out of the door.'

A female all right: Dallobar spotted her. 'Yeh,' he said.

'It ain't Mercy, though,' said Rip. 'I know who it is. It's a neighbour. She worries about Mercy bein' on her own and calls on her from time to time. It's sort of open house Mercy keeps. Maybe she's in town herself. That's Miz Cradow, Stella. A nice ol' body.'

There's hope for him yet, Dallobar reflected. And the Miner was sitting up and taking notice now.

'Let's go down.' Rip started off, the other two in the rear. The woman looked up and Rip waved. She could see them plain, waved back.

She had recognized Rip, and when the three men reined in, in front of her, she spoke the youngest one's name.

But she still looked kind of worried. A comely, plump lady in late middle age who'd obviously been relieved to see that the first rider of the trio was somebody she knew, whatever her personal opinion of him might be; but now she was uncertain of his companions.

'Mercy's not here,' she said, then paused.

'Mebbe she's gone to town,' said Rip.

'I told her I'd be callin' late this afternoon. She'd be keeping some preserves for me. The fire's gone out. Funny. Looks as if it's been doused. But Mercy usually keeps her oven warm. All the time. There are pies on the table ready to be baked ...'

It seemed that, in her nervousness, now she'd started she didn't want to give up on her talking.

'The back door was wide open. Mercy never locks her doors, 'cept at nights. I don't like her keeping 'em unlocked all day even when she goes into town, I've told her so, her bein' on her own an' all. But she says folks come in an' pick up things she's got ready for 'em. Her horse's gone, the little brown cob she calls Charlie, y'know....'

She ran down at last, looking from one to the

other of the three men as if seeking reassurance.

Dallobar said, 'Rip was bringing us to meet his sister. I'm Dan Dallobar and this old party is called the Miner 'cos that's what he used to be.'

The old-timer doffed his hat. 'Pleased to meet you, ma'am.'

The lady whom Rip had referred to as Miz Cradow was a mite easier now – Dallobar had that kind of effect on all kinds of females – and she said, 'You better come in.'

TEN

They didn't stay long. Not even for a cup of coffee.

Rip wanted to go to the neighbouring town, called Lone Canyon, though the nearest actual canyon of any kind was a couple of miles away.

Rip might have gone off half-cocked or anyway, hit the trail. But in which direction? Dallobar said, 'Think, boy.' So Rip thought; and still wanted to go to town. The Miner, too, said that was best. The girl might be there. Or somebody might know something.

The Miner was quite spry now. Miz Cradow seemed to have taken a shine to him, and she a married lady with kids as old as Rip or there-abouts. And she had to go home, supper to cook. The boys promised to call on her, give her news about Mercy, if they had any.

The smallholding had a look about it of having been quitted in a hurry, as if its occupants – if there had after all been more than one – were running from some impending natural disaster.

But the sun had gone and the air was balmy, cooler, and the ride to Lone Canyon was an easy one. Rip knew folks there, though some of the older ones looked at him somewhat askance.

But in a saloon they ran into an old muleskinner who had been a friend of the young man's parents. He said he had seen Mercy that afternoon.

'With a feller. Somebody I'd never see'd before and I know everybody in this territory. Riding side by side. Like Mercy knew him well. She see'd me, I'm sure o' that. But she didn't wave like she usually does.'

'Which way were they going?'

'Likely towards the border I guess. You an' Mercy in some sort o' trouble, son?'

'I don't think so,' Rip lied. 'What did that feller look like anyway?'

'My eyes ain't as good as they used to be. I can't cut a bug's ass with a whip like I useter. He was tall that feller, I guess, reckon that's all I can tell you about him.'

Rip gave the old man *dinero* for a drink and then the trio lit out.

'Why?' Rip said. 'Why?'

Nobody had an answer to that.

The Cap'n was dozing in the well-cushioned armchair behind the desk in the jail office when the discreet knocking on the back door impinged on his senses. He was instantly wide awake. Catnapping at bivouacs in his army days had given him this facility, and he figured he'd never want to lose it.

He picked up the Lightning Colt from the corner of the desk and, in the moccasins he had donned earlier, padded through the long, narrow corridor of the cell-block.

The back door was locked, bolted on the inside also. No need to leave it any other way now the birds had flown – all five of 'em – helped considerable by trickery and a measure of play-acting by folk who didn't usually operate that way.

The knocking came again, not loud, discreet, though much clearer to Marmaduke's ears now.

He leaned close to the door and said, 'Who is that?'

'It's me, Cap'n. Gilliver.'

Marmaduke unlocked and unbolted the door and opened it, not too wide, letting the dapper young man through the gap. Gilliver was the operative who had been left behind when the Cap'n had taken over a lawman's duties and the other two boys had tailed Dan Dallobar and the Miner.

The Cap'n had felt it best to leave one man behind in case he needed him. Gilliver had been hiding in a soddy just outside town, one of a few that nobody used now, not even Mexicans (and this was Mexican territory) or tame Indians.

He was only required to show himself if something untoward happened. He had opined that he didn't think anybody would recognize him, not many folks had gotten a good look at him before he was hauled off to the hoosegow with Dallobar and the other two.

'What's happened?' the chief demanded.

'Nothing, suh. Except that the other two boys are back. Two of 'em on one horse ...'

'How's that?'

Gilliver explained, concluding, 'I thought you ought to know.'

'I guess Dan knows what he's doing,' the Cap'n said. 'Thank you for putting me in the picture. You go back now.'

'Isn't much room for three of us in that soddy.'

'Find another one then. Now take it easy.'

Marmaduke Rayson locked and bolted the door behind the disgruntled operative and returned to his armchair.

He didn't feel like dozing any more. He felt he ought to be doing something, but he couldn't think of anything right then.

Even so, he was annoyed when more knocking occurred. But it was coming from the front door this time; and there were raised voices outside. The Cap'n got to his feet more quickly than he'd done last time. He made for the door, then turned, grabbed his Colt. He limped over to the door. He couldn't march any more, and that was something that oft times made his blood simmer.

And this, now, was one of those times.

He hadn't bothered to lock this door earlier. Gun in his right hand, he lifted the latch with his left, swung the door open.

It was Gilliver again, his face, flushed in the lamplight, wearing a mixture of expressions. Bewilderment, anger, but then, seeing his chief's now wrathful face, more than a small measure of bewilderment.

And behind him was an old-timer who poked a double-barrelled shotgun into his spine, propelling him towards the Cap'n, who had to step back.

'I catched him snoopin',' said the old gun-toter wrathfully. 'He's one of 'em who escaped. I seen him in the saloon in that ruckus. Hell, he poked me in the mouth with his elbow.'

There were more voices raised from behind the oldster. The Cap'n raised his pistol.

'No need for that cannon, friend,' he said.

At the voice of authority, the oldster lowered his weapon.

'Maybe he was coming to give himself up,' the Cap'n said.

'Yeh, I was,' said Gilliver. 'Yeh. Hell, I was only in a bar-room brawl, wasn't I? No need for all this fuss. I didn't want to get myself shot.'

'I'll take care of him,' the Cap'n said, raising his voice, peering past the oldster, who wasn't very big anyway.

The oldster backed. His *amigos* went the same way. But then one of them shouted again. And very likely! Coming down the street in the different lighting was the posse that had gone out after the jail-breakers. And the posse didn't have any prisoners.

'Get out my way, the lot of yuh,' bellowed the posse's leader, the heavy-set Sharper, who was already getting down from his horse.

ELEVEN

The three boys returned to Miz Cradow with their news. She was already on the stoop when they approached the small, neat ranch which was ablaze with light as if somebody was waiting for something to happen. But nothing had happened yet, and there were no revelations, just questions.

The visitors reined in cautiously as two more figures came out of the open door through which the yellow lights streamed. Both male. And the tall one had a shotgun in his hands, though its muzzles were sloped towards the ground.

'Light down, boys,' the man said. 'C'mon inside.'

The shorter, slimmer one, a boy of about thirteen, didn't say anything. He seemed to be staring at Dallobar's big hat.

Mr Cradow, Jim, was as affable as his missus. Neither of them was an oil-painting, but their boy, Simon, was bright-faced, intelligent-looking.

Dallobar said, 'Doesn't appear Miss Mercy was in town. But an old-timer saw her out past the place with a man and he says they seemed to be going border ways.'

'Can you describe that man?' asked Jim.

'I can do that,' said Rip Colen, almost roughly. He described Abel Teegle.

'I've seen him,' Miz Stella Cradow said. 'Didn't I see him with you one time, Rip?'

'Likely.'

'I've seen him since. On his own. He was leaving Mercy's place one afternoon when I called by.'

'I think I've seen him round these parts,' said young Simon. 'Once anyway.'

'He tipped his hat to me,' said the mother. 'Seemed a well-set-up sort of gent.'

'He is that,' said Rip sardonically.

'I don't think I've seen anybody like that,' said Jim in a disgruntled sort of way. He turned to his wife. 'Make some coffee for the gents, Stella.'

'I will.' She turned away.

'Don't bother, please, ma'am,' said Dallobar. 'We had somep'n in Lone Canyon. We'll be on our way.'

Simon was looking at the tall man, who grinned at him.

'That's a grand hat, mister,' Simon said. 'Where'd you get a hat like that?'

'Won it in a poker game.' That wasn't strictly

true. 'I wouldn't recommend tryin' to win a hat like this, though, partic'lerly in a poker game. Mugs! You lose more'n you win.'

'Listen to the man, son,' Jim said.

But the three visitors were soon on their way, promising to call again, though what the news might be then they had no notion.

'That boy surely took a shine to your hat, Dan,' the Miner said. 'You ought to've given it to him, an' then you could've gotten one like this'n of mine.'

'I wouldn't get buried in headgear like that,' Dallobar snorted.

Rip didn't join in the badinage. He was pushing his horse to the utmost. The other two kept up with him, both of them silent now. And it was Rip who finally spoke, shouting against a wind that was just getting up.

'I wonder how many times that bastard called on Mercy that I didn't know about.'

The jailhouse was a long, low adobe building. Sharper, a widower, whose only son was studying medicine up in Kansas City, occupied two spacious rooms and a kitchen on the edge of the structure and away from the cells. When he was around there was always a deputy on duty by the long cell-block, with its narrow passage and row of pens like tiny bedrooms with bunks and iron bars and small, barred high windows: a man

would need a ladder to look out and then he
wouldn't see much except the grimy backs of
town. A man would have to be a shrivelled midget
to be able to get out that way.

Callers usually came to the jail office. But if a
friend wanted to see Sharper particularly they
knocked on his own private door at the tail end of
the single-storey building. The burly man had an
early-morning caller while his new prisoner – one
he'd hoped he wouldn't have to see again, particularly in a cell – enjoyed his slumber.

Muttering imprecations, Sharper climbed out
of bed and, as the knocking came again, yelled,
'All right. All right, I'm comin'.'

A small Mexican youth stood at the door and
said, 'Good morning, Señor Sharper.'

'Good morning, Esteban. What's eating you?'

Esteban revealed a row of gleaming white
teeth. 'Don Miguel wishes for you to have break-
fast with him this morning, *señor*.'

'It's kinda early, *amigo*.'

'Don Miguel does not know time now, Señor
Sharper. It was just past dawn when he awoke
me with his bell.'

'C'mon in then. I'll be as fast as I can.'

Esteban knew that, despite his bulk, Sharper
could be very fast.

They were soon at the hacienda which was the
centre of the big rancho far out of town. The
grassland was lush and rolling out there.

The old Mexican don, whose legs were wasted and useless after a riding accident years before, greeted his old friend with his usual jovial courtesy, belying the pain in his eyes.

'I have things to tell you, Sharper,' he said. 'But first we must eat.'

It was an exhilarating spread laid out on a table as big as a ballroom and served by young ladies who moved soundlessly. Don Miguel was, like Sharper, a widower. He had two married daughters who lived over the border. His friends were legion and Sharper was one of very long standing.

Don Miguel was of old Spanish stock and his forebears had been in this territory far longer than those of his Anglo friends, including Sharper.

The old man rang the small silver bell that he carried attached to the thong of a quirt that he wore around his neck. Esteban appeared and pushed the soundless, ornate wheeled chair out on to the veranda; Sharper followed.

At a gesture from Don Miguel, Esteban remained with the two older men.

The Don said, 'I want to talk about the railroad robbery.'

Sharper said, 'You know about that.' It was a statement rather than a question. The old man got to know about pretty well everything that happened in his territory – and adjacent territory also, I'll be bound, the lawman thought.

'Of course I know. The stolen money was mine.'

'You never fail to surprise me, *amigo*,' Sharper said.

'We had an explosion in the silver mine.'

It wasn't a big mine but interestingly profitable and just another of the crippled old man's sidelines.

'I had to hire more people ...'

'Was anybody hurt?' Sharper asked.

'No, I am pleased to say. But there was a lot of damage which had to be cleared so digging can begin again. The money on the train was to pay those people. It wasn't as much as some folks expected.' The Don was smiling under his silver-grey moustache which, as Sharper remembered, had once been jet-black and fearsomely spiked and curled. 'There was more to come – to come here to the ranch, money to pay my people, to give them the greatest fiesta that they could ever imagine, with great gifts to all from me to them to celebrate my eightieth birthday.'

'I didn't know it was your birthday comin' up,' said Sharper. 'An' I didn't know you were that old.'

Don Miguel made a languid gesture. 'That money, the big money, was brought here the following day, in a cart with a few of my men. So the train robbers got the wrong day, the wrong information. The informant, a railroad man, a whelp, is out there,' a gesture of a long-fingered hand, 'in the courtyard. He has told us all we want to know. But you are the law, my friend, and I now want him to tell you.'

The old man turned to Esteban. 'Take Señor Sharper out there, set the man free and give him into the custody of the law.' He turned to Sharper again. 'I am sure you know much already. But I think you will learn more. I am sure you will.'

'I'm sure I will, yeh,' said Sharper and he followed Esteban out.

TWELVE

He was stripped to the waist and his body was scrawny and burned by the sun. The sun was out now but not yet very powerful. Sharper realized however that the way the man was placed the sun would get him most of the day. And at this time of the year the powerful rays could do plenty of harm to unprotected human flesh.

As the two men approached him, the figure, head on breast, seemed to be sleeping or unconscious; or dead. But then the face under the thinning hair was lifted; eyes looked in the direction of the visitors but did not seem to be seeing much.

The prisoner – and that he certainly was – had been spread-eagled on a wooden structure in the shape of a V. The sharp end was on the ground, or actually on a smallish block of wood. The man's arms spread upwards on the wider part of this huge, wooden letter; his arms were wound

around with rawhide and his wrists were teth-
ered.

He was so placed, so stretched, that his feet,
which were as bare as his torso, did not quite
touch the small wooden throne against which the
huge letter rested.

The body wasn't marked. The face didn't seem
to be marked either. There was something eerie
about this whole scene and Sharper did not like
it at all.

'Has he been tortured?' he asked.

'Not what I would call torture, *señor*,' Esteban
said. 'I have looked up at him and I have talked
to him. I have asked him questions and he has
answered them. I am sure that he has told us all
he knows. He was to come down this morning.'

The young man moved forward and reached for
a stone pitcher from the area near the base of the
contraption: that was the only name Sharper
could think to call it, if he called it anything at all.

From the back of his belt Esteban took a red-
and-white-spotted bandanna. He laved this with
water from the pitcher, then he reached up and
bathed the prisoner's face, having to stretch the
whole length of his arm in order to do so. He
seemed a strange, intelligent boy, almost as enig-
matic as his *jefé*, his mentor, who sat back there
in his wheelchair in the big hacienda.

Esteban gave the prisoner a drink but this
made him cough and splutter, the liquid running

from his slack lips and down on to his scrawny chest.

The young Mexican turned away. Carrying the pitcher he went over to a pump, slung the brackish water into the dust, and refilled the receptacle. People were moving out into the courtyard in the sunshine, none of them taking any notice of the scene which was being enacted in the centre of the wide space.

This time the prisoner drank. And Esteban was talking to him. But Sharper could not hear the words. The sun was becoming hotter.

From the back of his belt Esteban took a wicked-looking knife. He cut the prisoner's bonds. The man sagged. Sharper moved forward to help.

'He is yours now, *señor*,' Esteban said.

'I want him cleaned up before I take him anyplace,' Sharper said.

'The Don said you would want that,' Esteban commented with his white, flashing smile.

They helped the stumbling man across the courtyard.

Esteban said, 'When you are ready I will drive you and the man in the surrey. Your horse can trot behind.'

'He'll like that,' said Sharper.

Two girls went past and one of them gave the two men and their stumbling companion a curious glance. But she turned away quickly when Esteban gave her a blistering look in return.

This one has much power for a *caballero* so young, Sharper reflected. The stumbling man almost fell. They halted. Esteban looked back at the contraption in the middle of the courtyard and said:

'The Don's father used to have people whipped over there for all to see. The hacienda was much smaller then and the old man was considered by some to be a *bandido* and this an outlaw stronghold.'

That figures, Sharper reflected. He had heard horrible tales about the old *bandido*. A despot! Was his son a despot also? He could be. But he wore oftimes a coat of benevolence.

Esteban went in one direction with his charge and Sharper went another, rejoined Don Miguel. Now the prisoner was not mentioned, except for the crippled oldster to remark that all promises would be kept. Then they talked of older times which they both remembered, though Miguel's memory, of course, went much further back than his friend's did, to the times of legend and the tales that the older man knew as a boy.

Sharper, though visiting an old friend, had in the beginning as he accompanied Esteban the messenger, approached this place with a small feeling of trepidation. But this had long since gone and he was disappointed when Esteban returned sooner than expected to say that everything was ready.

The prisoner, whose name, it seemed, was Cathkart, was in the back of the surrey with his hands tied behind him. He was combed and brushed and wore fresh togs. He looked drowsy, though, and moved like an automaton.

This didn't prevent him, however, from flinging himself out of the surrey when they were well out on the trail.

This seemed to be more an act of petulance than defiance or desperation. He was soon recaptured. And Esteban said to him, sternly, 'You have made promises and they are promises you must keep. You know that, don't you, *amigo*?'

'I know that,' said the man, huskily, as he was hauled up on to the back of the surrey once more. It was the first time Sharper had heard the prisoner speak, though he and Esteban seemed to have some sort of understanding.

PART TWO

Daybreak

THIRTEEN

Jeremy Cathkart had had a different life once. Far different from the life he now lived and the things he was involved in now. A Southerner, he had been brought up on a plantation. As a boy his every need had been attended to by slaves. But the War, although he didn't remember any of it now, had changed everything.

His parents were dead. The plantation was just a dim memory that came and went like something in a fairy-tale. His only sister, trying to make a new life for herself, had married. She had died in childbirth.

Jeremy had been taken by what his parents had referred to as 'distant relatives', sharecroppers, 'poor whites'. When he was sixteen he had got out of there, had gone West as so many youngsters did in the uncertain times that came after civil war had torn a nation apart.

He worked in a dry-goods store and was fired

for stealing. He clerked, ran messages, swept floors, went out travelling as a drummer. He moved from job to job, stealing on the side at every opportunity. He wasn't cunning enough even for that. He earned himself a spell in a county jail for filching jewellery from an elderly lady who had been good to him.

In the great pond that was the lawless West, Jeremy Cathkart was a small fish that swam slowly and very erratically.

He called himself luckless. But suddenly, quite unexpectedly, that changed when he met an elderly gent in a bar. This gent took a shine to him and offered him a job. He took it. It was mundane clerical work, but it was on the railroad, something that most intelligent people said was up and coming, the flagship of a new generation which would leave the old West behind.

Jeremy's friend was a high muck-a-muck in railroad circles and it would be difficult to figure what he saw in young Jeremy. But he, the old feller, got himself killed by a runaway caboose careering down a slope and didn't have to worry any more. Jeremy didn't worry either: maybe he didn't have the capacity to do that any more. He was already a booze-hound. Soon he became a dope-hound as well.

He smoked his first opium pipe in the company of two Chinese track-workers in a soddy at the end of the line where almost everybody was celebrating in one way or another. He could always get opium, and various other concoctions after that. He tried other stuff that Italian workers got for him. He tried Indian stuff and peyote, and he drank a lot of pulque, mescal and tequila.

He was drunk when he first met Abel Teegle, who became a good friend of his; he knew Teegle was using him, but ol' Abe paid well for information and Jeremy wanted money all the while to help feed his habits.

But Abe let him down, that's how Jeremy looked at it. Then Don Miguel's boys picked him up and his worst experiences began and they were far worse than the blue devils, or any drug-induced nightmare.

The stringing-up. What else could you call it? The burning sun. Nothing to eat, and only a sip of water from time to time so that he would not get too dry and lose his voice. No booze; *no nothing*! It was all plumb sweated out of him.

And the monotonous insidious voice of the young man called Esteban, the questions, the promises of the horrible things that could happen to the flesh and the spirit of a man if the questions were not answered.

So the questions were answered. It was all told. And other promises made.

The big lawman had come. The one they called Sharper. Sharper had seen to it that his captive was cleaned, and fed, and even allowed a few glasses of tequila with the lemon and the salt, and Jeremy had promised again to keep his promises. And he had intended to do that.

Oh, he had tried to escape, had flung himself from the back of the surrey. But it had been a half-hearted attempt. He must have known it couldn't succeed....

The jail-cell welcomed him like a haven of peace. He even had a doctor to attend to his burned body and aching limbs and a small cut on his elbow that he had incurred when he fell from the surrey.

Oh, yes, he would keep his promises. Esteban had made that so. Drunk or not, he had always kept his ears open. Hell, Abe Teegle had *paid* him for that! He knew a lot about Abe as well. Abe was going to regret that he'd short-changed Jeremy Cathkart.

Sharper talked to Jeremy, told him things. And then Jeremy knew exactly what he had to do. And he told Sharper about the town called Daybreak.

Dan Dallobar and his two new friends rode pretty hard. But, despite Rip Colen's drive for furious haste, Dan took command, paced them and finally Rip saw the sense of this. As for the Miner, he tired more easily than he used to, admitted this. Besides, he'd been going along all the way with Dan even before he met up with fellow owlhooter, young Rip, again.

The young man had gone quiet, as if he were thinking deeply. And finally he came out with it.

'Whether Mercy's gone with Teegle willingly or not, I think I know where he might well be takin' her.'

'Where's that, son?' the Miner asked. His manner towards his erstwhile young partner had grown ever more avuncular as the trail lengthened.

Dallobar reflected that this was the first time that Rip had half-admitted that his sister might have gone with Teegle of her own free will. Rip would know more about Teegle's romantic attributes than Dan did – and womenfolk were kind of peculiar creatures anyway. He'd known more than a few, and knew that he, for some reason, had a way with them. Yeh, he'd had his way with 'em all right – but he still couldn't figure any of 'em right out.

He almost missed Rip's answer to the Miner's question. It rose above the sound of the horses' hoofs.

'A little town called Daybreak,' Rip said.

'Funny name for a town,' the Miner said.

Dallobar took it up. 'A hellhole on the border. The Mexes, Indian tribes, *mestizos* an' the like call it something different. Hell's bells, they all seem to have different sorts of name for it.

'Jaw-breakin'. It's the Americanos who called it Daybreak – sort of a translation they thought it was, I guess, an' that stuck.'

'I heard Abe mention it a coupla times,' Rip said. 'Reckoned he had a lot o' friends there.'

'It's an outlaw town all right,' Dallobar said. 'I only visited it once but I figured what it was all right.'

He didn't go on to tell them that he'd tracked a killer there but hadn't been able to bring the man back alive like the Cap'n had wanted. The man was a fast professional gunfighter, had wanted it the other way and Dan had had to satisfy, and kill him with one bullet to the brain.

'We're on the right trail for that, ain't we, Dan?' Rip asked.

'I guess so. But we got a fair way to go yet.'

They'd asked along the trail but nobody seemed to have had any sightings of the girl and man. It was pretty evident that, if they'd passed this way, they hadn't halted where anybody could take a good look at them. But what, if anything, that signified, the trio who followed them couldn't figure.

FOURTEEN

Sharper had reckoned that another day wouldn't make any difference. And Cathkart could rest up more. He was mending quicker than had been expected, even the doc admitted that. In fact, after talking a blue streak to Sharper, getting less tired, he'd even become chirpy.

He'd show them as well, he'd said, he'd show 'em a lot!

If he wants to ride, let him ride then, the doc said.

So they set out by night. Part of this was because the dapper, ex-jailbird operative, Gilliver, was going with them and Sharper didn't want *him* spotted.

Esteban had stayed in town rather than returning to the rancho. He also was going with the posse, as was Deputy Tubs.

Captain Marmaduke Rayson was going to stay at the jailhouse, seemed to get a kick out of that, said it favoured his bad leg, whatever that meant; you never could tell with the ol' Cap'n the now unjailed Gilliver said.

They picked up Gilliver's two ex-jailbird colleagues at the place where they'd been hiding and they became part of the posse also.

By then Sharper figured he'd got enough. Good men. Professionals. All except Cathkart, although by then he was beginning to act that way.

Esteban kept an eye on him all the time....

Teegle had confessed to Mercy that the riches he had weren't quite as plentiful as he'd expected them to be, an unfortunate circumstance that he hadn't been able to overcome. But then again, riches there were, hers and his – and a grand life ahead for both of them.

He hadn't confessed that in order to get all of the riches he had had to kill one man and leave another to die, both men who had trusted him.

Now he was uncertain, and uncertainty didn't sit well with him. But he couldn't go back. He couldn't take Mercy back. Had her brother, Rip, survived after all? He hadn't been struck by a sidewinder. But there were other poisonous things whose venom could cause death – and Rip had looked pretty far gone.

He'd sort of liked Rip. Now he decided he

should've killed the boy anyway, making sure.

He wondered whether he'd ever mentioned Daybreak to Rip, couldn't remember doing that. Did Rip know the place anyway? But whether the answer to that was yes or no was of little account now.

When they got to Daybreak he took Mercy to Ma Dodds' place, which was the best lodging house he knew in a town that wasn't noted for its amenities, particularly of the sort that catered to respectable young ladies. He left Mercy with the elderly lady, knowing Ma would look after her like a hen with a new chick. He had a cup of coffee with them before leaving, on business he said, but he wouldn't be away long.

He hadn't been any other place since entering town, had made a beeline for Ma Dodds' place first of all.

He had left his horse with an ancient hostler who ran the dirtiest, smelliest stables of the lot, and right on the edge of town at that. Mercy's mount had been stashed at another place. She had seemed to find this strange but hadn't commented on the fact. She seemed to be with Abe all the way now.

He got his horse back now and borrowed a short digging tool from the old souse. The man hadn't remembered Abe Teegle, though he'd seen him more than once, time back. He wouldn't remember lending out the tool either or who he'd

lent it to: a man who gave him more greenbacks
so he could stagger to the nearest cantina and
imbibe more of the yellow liquid he loved so
much.

Abe Teegle rode out to a rocky place he knew,
not seeing anybody in the failing light. He skirted
a grove of cottonwoods and came upon the rocky
place he remembered; he had buried loot there
before years ago, and recovered it intact later. He
dug. He rolled rocks over the place after he'd
dropped the railroad money snugly into it. He left
no signs, no footmarks or anything else.

Satisfied, he rode back to town. He threw the
digging implement in to the old booze hound's
place but now went on from there and stashed his
horse in with Mercy's mount.

He went on quickly, afoot, to his cousin's place,
the biggest rathskellar in Daybreak. Cousin Bret
was a big man also, in more ways than many, had
a slew of hardcases at his beck and call.

He hadn't expected Abe so soon, though one of
his boys had said he thought he'd seen Abe a
while ago, hadn't mentioned any woman though.
Abe felt a small pang of alarm, wondering if the
gabby hardcase had done any tailing. Didn't seem
like it though. He didn't of course tell Bret about
the money, just about the girl. Bret said bring her
over and Abe said he would.

Night had fallen. Abe went back to Mercy
quickly. She stood by the lighted window. Ma

Dodds had fixed a meal. They had lamb stew with carrots, peas, shredded onions, brown beans, a savouring of chilli and, on the side, whole potatoes baked in their skins and served with a salad concoction, the ingredients of which Ma didn't specify. But Abe told the beaming old lady that she hadn't lost her touch.

To follow they had some cheese Mrs Dodds, widowed and childless and a picker-up of stray dogs both animal and human, had made herself. And some of her cold cherry-pie, and coffee, and bourbon. And then Ma and Abe smoked a strong-smelling cheroot which Mercy declined, saying she had had her fill of everything and it had been glorious

Abe, not saying it aloud, reflected that Ma was an even better cook than Mercy; and he had had a couple of meals back at her place not so long ago.

Young Rip had first introduced Abel Teegle to his sister as a travelling cattle-buyer, had called him the chief, the straw-boss.

Abe had called on the widowed girl a few times on his own, hadn't told Rip about this, didn't think Mercy could have either.

With Mercy, Abe played his Southern gentleman role and, surprising himself, found this easier to do than usual. Mercy was getting under his skin. He didn't think he had ever thought about any woman before the way he thought about her; more and more he thought about her.

She had left everything for him, just let it lie. Only later did he begin to think that that hadn't been good, might make folk come after them.

But it was too late to worry about that now. And here they were at Ma Dodds' place and she, who had an open heart for 'most everybody, was treating them like honoured guests. Sitting with these two good women in the lamplight was to Abel Teegle like something from an old dream....

But could it last? He looked at Mercy and said, 'In a bit, honey, I want you to come with me and meet an old friend of mine.'

'I guess you're going to take her to your cousin, Bret Toler's place, huh?' said Ma Dodds.

'I am. But you know Bret, Ma. He can be a prime gentleman when he chooses. Nobody messes with him. Me neither.'

The old frontiers-woman looked at the girl and said, 'You can bank on that, Mercy child.'

'Thank you, Ma,' said Teegle. 'Anyways, first off I reckon I ought to go get me a shave and a wash-up, a proper do-over.'

'I wonder you didn't do that soon as you got here,' said the old lady tartly, "stead o' just a splash like a drunk with a headache.'

'I had more important things to do. But now I'm goin' – I'm goin' I tell yuh.'

'Well, the bathhouse is on'y two doors away.'

'I know where the bathhouse is.'

Teegle took his leave. They heard the outer door close behind him. The place was quiet then. Earlier, folk had been leaving for their night out. To Mercy, away from the quietness of her own place – far away now – some of the sounds seemed kind of menacing.

But Abe had told her that Ma Dodds never stood for any nonsense, was well respected by some of the hardest folk alive in this town, which was of the sort that Westerners termed 'wide open'.

Earlier, while Abe had been out, Mercy had taken a bath in a tin tub in a small bedroom adjacent to Ma's own more palatial quarters. The water had been carried to her by a pretty young half-breed girl called Jaco whom Mercy hadn't seen since. For some obscure reason – as it seemed to Mercy anyway – Ma had remarked that she knew some rough characters of all stripes and sexes but she didn't run a bawdy house.

Now, as the two women sat in the spacious, well-lit Western kitchen, the older one said, 'You know Abe's an outlaw, don't you, honey?'

The girl's reply was slow in coming, and hesitant.

'He – he buys cattle.'

'Oh, he handles cattle all right, I wouldn't wonder,' said Ma. 'Among other things.'

Mercy still seemed to be groping for words, her dark eyes uncertain.

Ma went on: 'I think he came from good stock an' somep'n went wrong. He treats you good, I can tell that. Good stock. They all say that. I've got all kinds here, honey, and I treat 'em fair. So Abe handles cattle.' She gave a little spurt of genuine laughter. 'And I sew wimples for nuns. And there are no nuns in Daybreak and I never could stitch worth a damn. My old man used to say that cookin' an' lovin' were my best things.'

The front door slammed as folks came in. There was more banging, and voices rang out in altercation. The old lady bustled to the kitchen door and flung it open.

'Quit that!' she shouted

'Sorry, Ma,' a loud male voice said. A woman giggled. But there was quiet after that.

But that wasn't enough for Miz Dodds. 'Get that hussy out o' here,' she said.

The younger female voice started up again but was drowned by the male voice that told her to shut her face. A second male voice said, 'All right, Ma.' There was the sound of the door being opened again and then slammed shut. And quiet again. And the old lady, returning to her seat, said, 'Have another cup o' coffee, honey.'

'All right.'

Abel Teegle came back. He'd been pretty quick.

'Don't he look purty now?' said Ma.

The girl smiled uncertainly, didn't say anything.

'You ready, Mercy?' Abe asked.

Mercy went up to her own little room to fetch her things.

FIFTEEN

Marmaduke Rayson was dozing when somebody knocked on the door. He immediately came fully awake, lifting the gun from the corner of the desk, getting to his feet, limping across the office, drawing the door-bolt, raising the gun as he opened the door, letting out a gush of light which illuminated the face of the single man who stood there.

An old face. Clean and shining, but wrinkled. A slouch hat that looked brand-new. Pretty good togs.

A pause. Then Marmaduke gave a little whoop.

'By all that's holy. Uncle Tally.'

'Evenin', Cap'n.'

The door was opened wide and the visitor entered He was bow-legged, shorter than Marmaduke. Considerably older too, though the Cap'n was no chicken.

'I was tol' you wuz 'ere, didn't believe it at first. You turned sheriff or somep'n?'

'Just temporary. How long you been out?'

'Few days. I came to see Sharper. He put in some good words for me, got me earlier release than I'd expected.'

'He got you in there in the first place, didn't he?'

'I don't blame 'im for that.'

Tally had never been a huge success as a bandit. He and two pards had tried to stick up an express office, not knowing there was a sizeable bunch of armed guards inside watching over the loot the outlaw trio coveted. There hadn't been any shooting, nobody was hurt. Three got roped. Sharper had taken over.

'What's happened to the other two, Uncle?' Marmaduke asked.

'One's still in. Extra time. He busted a guard's jaw. The younger boy came out with me. We parted company then. He went back to his family. Say, I heard about that train robbery, Cap'n. Us jailbirds do get to know things, y'see. How you doin', ol' hoss!'

'Not so bad, old friend. Not bad at all, Uncle.'

Tally wasn't Marmaduke's real uncle. They had served together in the war. Tally was actually Dan Dallobar's uncle, had saved that boy's bacon time back. He'd then introduced the young big boy to his old chief, Marmaduke, who then, as now, ran a range-detective outfit. That was when, cheerfully, Marmaduke had began to call his old soldier-pard Uncle Tally, just as big Dan did.

Marmaduke now brought out the hooch from the cupboard in the wall where Sharper always kept it. The two men sat opposite each other, toasted each other, grinning like a couple of happy cats.

'I heard that Sharper left town an' so did young Dan,' Tally said. 'I didn't get the full story, though.'

Marmaduke told him the story from his side, including the information that had been gotten from the railroad sneak called Cathkart.

'Daybreak,' said Tally. 'I know the place. It's purty well run by that feller named Bret Toler who is Abe Teegle's cousin or somp'n close. If Dan an' Sharper an' the rest are on their way there an' they get there afore the posse …'

'They're bound to I guess,' put in the Cap'n.

'If Teegle's there he'll have plenty to back 'im. Those boys will be goin' into a hotbed o' trouble. I'm gonna go that way.'

'You sure?'

'I'm sure.'

'Wish I was coming with you.'

'You cain't be in two places at once, ol' hoss. I'll go quick. Mebbe I can catch up with that posse.'

'You had eats?'

'Yes. I'll get a few supplies.' Tally rose. 'Sorry

this has been such a short visit. I'll get back to you.'

'I hope you will.'

'Bank on it, ol' chief. I'm a goddam fool, but I'm l'arnin'. Mebbe I can do somep'n straight an' right this time.'

They shook hands, then Tally made his bow-legged way out of the office, the Cap'n watching him go down the street in the lights until he disappeared into a late-open store.

It was a busy night in Daybreak. The lamps sputtered and blazed, and hissed in the quiet parts. But there weren't many quiet parts now, and Mercy and Abe were walking towards the noisy area, towards the sounds of voices and thumping, and the clatter of hoofs, with, now and then, the jangling of a badly-tuned piano cutting in.

They approached a long two-storey building which seemed to be constructed of a mixture of adobe – the Mexican and border standby – and weathered clapboard.

Shouting rannies were hitching their horses at a long hitching rail which was broken in the middle by a short flight of hollowed wooden steps which led up to the almost dangerous-looking plank sidewalk. High-heeled riding boots made a horrendous noise, awakening echoes resounding even over the general devilish din.

To Mercy, far away from her quiet, industrious

days on the smallholding, there was a frightening menace in what she saw before her, and the sounds she heard. Her own town had seen some festive times but never anything like this. This had a quality of violence about it, of menace.

Looking in the direction the man and the girl approaching on foot, a big feller in a wide-awake hat yelled something and the partner at his side screeched with laughter. Another man said something sharply and the pair shut up, followed the rest of the bunch through the swinging batwings; there was a gush of yellow light, an outburst of louder noise, the piano clanking, rising, dimming....

'We turn up here to the side door,' Teegle said.

Mercy went with him docilely: there was little else she could do.

Light spilled out from a narrow window, but in the main the alley was in darkness, and was pretty narrow also.

The two men came as if from nowhere, the jumbled noises covering their approach from behind. Teegle turned swiftly. Both men had guns, the blue steel gleaming in the fragmented yellow light from the narrow window.

'What do you want?'

Teegle wasn't allowed another word. One man was a little in front of the other. He lashed out with the gun and the barrel caught Teegle solidly on the side of a head: the dull thud could be heard even over the other sounds. Teegle made a short, broken sound and fell away from the girl, hitting the wall opposite the lighted window and slumping down against it, unconscious.

Mercy opened her mouth to scream but the gun-swinger's partner was too quick for her, clapping his hand brutally over her mouth, his other arm around her, his fingers digging into her breast.

She felt as if she was being stifled to death. A ball seemed to swell in her throat, another one in her body. She tried to bite the clutching fingers. She couldn't. She threshed against the other cruel hand, but to no avail. Suddenly there was no light any more, only Stygian blackness, and a rushing noise, and then only the blackness, nothing else....

SIXTEEN

They had ridden hard in the coolness of the night and now the first flush of dawn was beginning to appear in the skies ahead. Horses and men were tired but looked at the skies, got ready to welcome the dawning light. The men made reassuring noises to their cayuses and looked ahead. All except the ex-railroad character, Cathkart, who suddenly fell off the dun mare that had been hired for him back in town. A dull thud. A still body.

Men had been dozing in the saddle: accomplished riders, they had been accustomed to doing this on long trails.

Even Esteban had given up watching Cathkart, after pegging him as a poor horseman, easy to catch if he tried to make a break.

The man had been keeping his promise, however, had even reined up beside Sharper from

108

time to time and pointed the way.

Esteban got down by the man, who began to groan and stir, moving his head restlessly from side to side as blood trickled sluggishly from his hairline.

One of the range operatives who had joined the posse helped the Mexican youth to get Cathkart back in the saddle. Then Esteban remounted his own horse, nudged it close to Cathkart's and held him up.

'What did I do,' the man mumbled. 'What did I do?' Somebody laughed. Nobody answered the question.

Sharper said, 'It's time we rested anyway, gave the hosses a break.' He pointed. 'We'll bivouac in that grove of trees ahead.'

They lit a small fire, brewed coffee, ate hardtack and biscuits, lolled and smoked while the horses browsed, cropping the grass away from the small flames.

They were still there when the horseman came out of the red sun.

Sharper saw him. 'Jumpin' cats. If that ain't Tally,' he carolled.

'It is.' The oldster slid down from the saddle. The two men shook hands. Explanations were short after Tally told Sharper that he'd already called on the Cap'n.

Esteban had bandaged Cathkart's head and said jocularly that the man would live but was in

such a state that he could well fall off his nag
again.

'Some guide!' snorted Sharper.

'I can guide you to Daybreak,' Tally said.

It was down to Esteban who kneeled in front of
the half-reclining Cathkart and said, 'I guess it's
not far now to Don Miguel's place. Can you ride
to there?'

'Ye-es.'

'Do that then. The Don will not harm you now;
he will give you work. You have kept your
promises.' Esteban looked back at Sharper, the
leader of the party.

The older man nodded his head. 'All right,' he
said, 'let 'im go.'

They watched him go, obviously striving now
to keep himself upright in the saddle. The dun
mare wasn't a frisky creature anyway.

'All right,' said Sharper. 'Let's move!'

Tally ranged himself beside his old sparring
partner; and Sharper said, 'Glad to have you
back.'

'It's down to you I'm back so soon, *amigo*.'

Rip Colen said, 'Not too far to go now.'

Dan Dallobar said, 'I guess.'

The Miner said, 'Jesus, my achin' back!'

Rip said, 'I know a nice place in Daybreak
where you can lie down, old-timer. A nice lady
who'll look after you prime.'

'I ain't about to lie up in no whorehouse, son. Hell, I wouldn't have the energy right now. Still an' all, if'n you …'

Rip interrupted with an explosive burst of laughter. 'Not at all, you ol' jackass. Not that at all. Hell, if ol' Ma Dodds heard what you just said she wouldn't allow you on the front stoop, or out back with the coyotes I shouldn't wonder. She keeps the best place in town. But she's tough, I'll tell you.'

Dallobar said, 'Wait a minute. I think I remember that name. Ma Dodds. I only visited Daybreak briefly just once an' would likely get lost now if I tried to find it on my lonesome. I stayed just overnight an' I guess my landlady was Ma Dodds. A seasoned frontier lady an' one of the best cooks I've come across in my travels, yes, sir.'

'That's her all right.'

But it was late afternoon when they came in sight of Daybreak. Rip Colen pointed it out triumphantly as he squinted against the red sun going down over the sprawling collection of buildings lying in a small valley with a narrow creek between it and the three horsemen. The town looked quiet. Would they find here what they were looking for? They went slowly now, three saddle-tramps after a long ride. Quiet now. Sober. After his good-natured joshing of the Miner, Rip's manner was melancholy now, his head bent as if, with his sombre eyes, he was watching his horse's hoofs, their monotonous but inevitable progress....

Ma Dodds greeted the young owlhooter cheerfully. But then her expression sobered, only lightening a little when she recognized Rip's tall companion.

'You've got a good memory, Ma,' Dallobar said.

'It helps a lot in this business,' said the old lady. 'But who could forget a handsome bucko like you?'

'Horsefeathers,' said the Miner, not wanting to be left out.

'And who is this old gentleman?' said Ma, somewhat tartly.

She was introduced to the Miner who, with a sidelong glance at Rip, said, 'Don't tell 'er what I said.'

'What was that?'

An explanation wasn't forthcoming. And Rip had become quiet again, the old lady suddenly seeming to take a pattern from him, asking another question.

'You lookin' for your friend, Abe Teegle, young feller?'

'I figured I'm to see him in Daybreak, yeh.'

'He was right here with me,' Ma said. 'Him an' a pretty little girl called Mercy.'

'That's my sister. Where are they now?'

'I don't know. I expected 'em back after they went out last night. But I ain't seen 'em since.'

'I'll go lookin',' said Rip.

It was almost full dark by now. But Dallobar said, 'Leave it a while. Till more folk are about. Not to call too much attention to ourselves.'

'Yeh, I guess that'd be best,' said Rip reluctantly.

'We'll wash up.'

'I'll get you somep'n to eat,' Ma said.

Afterwards, as they sat at the table, partaking of the chow that the old lady had produced in double-quick time she told them where she thought Mercy and Abel had gone first off last night.

'That figures,' said Rip grimly.

He was again raring to go. And his two friends were with him all the way now, rising.

'Take care, boys,' Ma said.

SEVENTEEN

Cousin Bret Toler had sworn that if Abe didn't tell him where the loot was by that evening he'd let his boys do what they wanted with the girl and then finish her.

Abe said there wasn't as much as he and his boys had figured; but the boys were out of it now and he would give Bret a split for his help, a safe trip over the border for him and Mercy, a new life.

Bret said he wanted it all, he'd been planning a new life himself, the pickings here weren't what they used to be and he was tired of the place, tired of the Western life, wanted to go East, start again: the money from Abe would come in right handy.

Abe tried to play on family feelings, but this didn't work. Bret was as cruel and ruthless as he, Abe, had been himself: what else had he expected for Godsakes?

For all Abe knew, Mercy could already be dead.

He had never felt for any other girl the way he'd felt for her.

He agreed to do what Bret said. Maybe he could pull something after all. So they went out into the burgeoning night, five of them all told. Big odds against one unarmed man. Weapons. Digging implements. A man on watch from the cottonwoods while, past them, the others moved rocks, dug.

'You're family,' Bret said at length. 'I'll let you go, you an' the girl, go wherever you like, except if I see you here again I'll shoot you on sight.'

'Hell, not you. You won't. You'd get your stinkin' boys to do it.'

'Let him dig,' barked Bret and one of the men handed Teegle a shovel. Immediately Teegle swung it at his cousin. Not quick enough, though. Toler backed, laughed harshly. At safe distance, he watched Teegle and another man work while others stood with drawn guns.

Teegle knew that he was near to the loot he had buried. But what then? Would Bret have him shot and then buried in the convenient hole before it was covered again?

The man who was working beside Teegle straightened up, clutching his side, his face twisted.

'I've done enough,' he said. 'My side where a hoss kicked me, Bret, it's playin' up. Let somebody else have a go.'

Bret motioned to the man with the gun to take over. Bret had his own gun in his hand now. Maybe he felt he might have kind of outsmarted himself in giving a desperate man a potential weapon, a shovel, which he might use for something other than the purpose it was made for.

This thought flashed through Teegle's mind. He took a desperate bet on it. As the man with the twisted back turned away from him, Teegle swung his weapon, caught the hardcase solidly on the back of the head, pitching him to the dust. He swung at the second man, who'd backed; he missed him.

From behind, Bret fired his weapon. The slug hit the blade of the shovel, clanged, whined away into nothingness.

Teegle's hand was forced down at the impact of the bullet on steel. He was trying to lift the improvised weapon, seeing out of the corner of his eye that Bret was trying to get in another shot without hitting his own man. But this fellow, charging forward, got more in the way than ever. He was too quick for Teegle though, swinging his gun whiplike. The gleaming steel barrel caught its man a glancing blow on the side of the head. Teegle sank dazedly to the ground.

Mercy had been locked in a small room which had no window but, high in the tall walls, were gratings which let in air but couldn't possibly act as any kind of escape hatch. The place was not like a cell. It was in fact well appointed. There were a bed, two chairs, one of them very comfortable, with padded back and arms; a dressing-table with a complete toilet set, and a small pump in the corner which gushed water into a drain when manipulated. It looked like a place that another woman could have occupied before Mercy was put there.

She had seen the unconscious Abe taken away, but nobody had done her any harm after she was taken from the man who'd first clutched her. He had been told off by his boss, who introduced himself to her as Bret Toler, Abe's cousin.

He said this mockingly, his white teeth flashing beneath his handsome black moustache. He had a fancy gambler's waistcoat.

He said she would be treated with the utmost courtesy if she behaved herself. He said that nobody could hear her if she screamed. But he added that if she did make any noise his men might come in and he personally wouldn't interfere with anything they might choose to do to her. He wouldn't tell her why Abe had been attacked and herself imprisoned. He just would not answer any of her questions.

There were two men outside the stout door, she knew this. They had been there all night.

Her emotions changed slowly but inevitably. First terror, then bewilderment, almost a disbelief in what had happened (as if it were a nightmare or something); then anger as she told herself she was strong and given a chance she could fight. No one should be allowed to do *this* to her.

She even slept. When she rose, still in her somewhat dishevelled clothes, she went over to the door, rapped on it lightly and said, 'Is there anybody there?'

'Shut up, lady,' a voice answered. 'Or it'll be worse for you.'

The voice sounded sort of drowsy, as if its owner had been awakened. She had no means of knowing the time. Maybe it was earlier than she'd calculated.

The room was illuminated by a hanging hurricane-lantern which gave very adequate light. Mercy had, earlier before she went to sleep, searched the place for some kind of weapon – something club-like, or sharp – but without success.

She started to look again, now going down on her hands and knees, not caring a fig about her dignity. It was when rising from this position, beneath the dressing-table, that her eyes fell on the wash basin. She had already inspected the large earthenware jug, found it too heavy and cumbersome, too awkward to swing through an open door. But the bowl in which the ewer stood was another matter. It could be swung sideways through a door which was not completely open.

She moved the ewer to the floor. She lifted the bowl. It was, she thought, somewhat lighter than the ewer. But, even without a handle, it was easier to manage and, held sideways, to swing.

I'm no pantywaist, male or female, the girl reflected, I've handled heavier things than this.

Now her mind was working fast. She had a brainwave. Carrying her heavy weapon – and that's what it was now – she went over to the door. Resting the bowl against her, she hammered on the door with her fists and screamed at the top of her lungs, shutting from her mind the things Bret Toler had said, his horrendous threats.

Outside, a man shouted. Just the one voice. She screamed, 'There's a rat! Let me out, there's a big rat! ... Please let me out.' She was gasping now, sobbing, making begging, piteous sounds.

She heard the key turn in the lock on the other side of the door. She lifted the heavy earthenware bowl, held it sideways, aiming it at the edge of the door.

The door opened. She saw the man, his belt, the belly hanging over it. She swung the bowl with all her force, felt the edge of it dig into flesh. With her shoulder she thrust the door open wider.

The man was bent over, gasping. One hand fumbled for the butt of his gun. Mercy lifted the big bowl right way up and brought it down on the unprotected head. Over the man's shoulder she had been able to note that there wasn't anybody else about.

The bowl didn't break, was too tough. But the man lay on his face, didn't move. Blood seeped through his thinning hair.

Mercy dropped the bowl, bent over and yanked the unconscious guard's Colt from its holster. He might be dead. She couldn't stop to find out.... What the hell...! She hefted the gun. She'd handled one of these. Her husband had had one. It was back at the ranch.

She was in a stone passage. Ahead of her was another door, to which she crossed. She lifted the latch, pushed; the door opened.

She was surprised to find that it was dark. She'd lost track of time all right while she was in that fancy cell.

She welcomed the dark. There was no moon that she could see. She could look out, though; any Western townie could recognize what she saw. Privies, rubbish dumps, weeds, scrub grass, vegetation further back and a dark expanse; no lights at all. The 'backs' of town.

She paused, but only momentarily. There could be danger behind. She figured the way to go, hoped she was right. Gun in hand, she moved forward, her eyes roving as she became more accustomed to the dark.

She wasn't sure whether she would be able to recognize the back of Ma Dodds' place. She wouldn't risk going round the front from which noises came intermittently to her ears.

She crouched back against a wall when a back door opened, letting out a gush of light. A man crossed to a privy. She waited for the door of this to close before she went on, passing through the band of yellow light. A little later she paused again next to a kitchen window from which light spilled. She had passed other kitchens like this but not one so bright before. Also she had already judged that this was about the right place. She remembered that Ma had said that she never locked her doors until she was ready for bed.

Mercy tried the door and it opened.

The bright kitchen was empty. But then the old lady came through the communicating door and her hand flew to her mouth when she saw the girl, the gun in her hand.

'It's all right, Ma.'

'Where've you been, Mercy? And where's Abe?'

'I don't know where Abe is now.'

They both sat down, Mercy placing the gun on the kitchen table near to her elbow.

'Your brother's been here,' Ma said.

'Rip?'

'Yes. With a big feller named Dan Dallobar and an old man they call the Miner. They were lookin'' for you. I guess they've gone down to Bret Toler's place.'

'I've been there,' said Mercy caustically.

She told her story.

Then she added, 'I ought to go find those boys.'

'They can look after themselves,' Ma said sternly. 'You stay here. Wait. There's somebody I want you to meet.'

'All right.' Somewhat mystified, Mercy waited.

She heard the old lady climbing the stairs, marvelled at how fast she moved.

Then two pairs of footsteps, coming back.

When Ma came into the kitchen she had another lady with her, younger than Ma but not much, handsome, with long hair, wearing a long, fluffy robe.

'This is Grace. She lives upstairs. She's a retired lady. Tell Mercy about the room, Grace.'

'I was there for a fortnight,' Grace said, sitting primly on the edge of a chair while Ma remained standing, looking down at the two.

'I was locked in like you. But it was an arrangement that Bret made with me. Men used to visit me, y' know. Is there a panel in the middle o' that door now?'

'I didn't see any panel.'

'Well, honey, there was one then. It was bolted on the inside. Men used to knock on the door and I used to open the panel and look at 'em and if I fancied 'em I'd let 'em in, using the key Bret had sold to them. If they took the key back without coming in they got their money back. I was sort of the business y'know. But I got sick o' being cooped up so I stopped the business. I ain't been back to anything like that since. Have I, Ma?'

'Not to my knowledge, Grace.'

'I have to tell you, though, Miss Mercy, Bret Toler treated me fair. He can be a savage bastard, though, if he puts his mind to it.'

'Thank you for telling me all this, Grace,' Mercy said.

'No mind, honey. Now I'm gonna put my togs on an' go look for your brother, Rip, an' his friends like Ma told me. I remember Rip. I remember Abe Teegle as well. Maybe I'll even run into him.'

'Oh ... take care, Grace.'

'Nobody's gonna mess with me!'

She was back sooner than they expected and with her was the trio she'd gone out to find.

Dan Dallobar had to admit that they hadn't seen hide nor hair of Abel Teegle, or even Bret Toler. They hadn't pushed their luck too far in Toler's place, which was known as the Golden Calf. They'd been told that Toler was out of town.

'Helluva lot of his friends in that place,' said the Miner. 'We'd need more firepower if'n ...' He let things tail off.

The men were scandalized to hear what had happened to Mercy. Then again it could've been worse, as the girl herself affirmed. So they persuaded Rip not to go off half-cocked.

EIGHTEEN

Toler and the rest came in the back way. They still had Abe Teegle with them, battered, unsteady on his legs. He had a swelling lump on his head which he'd collected when Mercy and he had been attacked in this very alley. He also had a weal on the other side of his cranium where one of the boys had slugged him back in the diggings. This particular boy was now carrying the boodle.

Nobody knew exactly what was to be done about Teegle, not even Toler, who couldn't seem to be able to make his mind up; a wonder for him, though he could be temperamental, enraged even about small things.

And he was now walking into something which would enrage him somewhat, being met at the back door by an expostulating, almost cringing hardcase who told him that the girl Mercy had escaped.

'Where were you?'

'I had to go to the privy, boss. Had to! I left Beezer at the girl's door. She got to him somehow, slugged him. Bad. He's in bed.'

'Where's the girl to?'

'I don't know, boss.'

Abe Teegle started to laugh, a strange gulping sound. The enraged Toler drew his gun, but he didn't turn it on his cousin, he slashed out with it at the cringing hardcase and caught him on the hairline with murderous force. The man went down so hard he almost bounced. But then he lay still, curled up, and Toler said 'Leave him' and they all stepped over him.

Another man accosted them, said a feller called Dan Dallobar had been in the Golden Calf.

'I remember him. A gunfighter. He wuz askin' about this one,' he gave a jerk of a thumb in Abe Teegle's direction, 'but nobody told 'im nothin'. He had with him this feller's pard, the snotty-nosed young 'un called Rip, an' an old-timer I didn't recognize. Somebody's tol' me since that these boys met up with that old whore called Grace who used to be here; and they went with her.'

'Grace lives now in Ma Dodds' place,' one of the returning party said.

Another said, 'Mebbe the girl's gone there, Bret.'

'Likely,' said the boss, back on even keel it seemed. He pointed at Abe Teegle. 'Put him to bed. Guard him. I want no more slip-ups or heads will roll, I'm telling you. We might need this one.'

126

He meant his cousin, who didn't seem to be taking much interest in the proceedings now, not showing his face much. 'All of you wait,' Toler went on. He took the boodle from the man who'd carried it.

He went into his spacious, well-appointed office and put the money in the safe. He was the only one who knew the combination.

He returned to the waiting hardcases. 'I want a couple more men,' he said. 'Then we're going to Ma Dodds' place.'

There were two more volunteers. He split his band up, out front, out back, the latter having to step over the man who lay just inside the doorway. He wasn't dead, was moaning now.

'Drag him in f' Chrissakes,' barked the leader, and this was done.

The three men and three women were in Ma Dodds' comfortable sitting-room taking coffee, all of them wondering what was going to happen next.

Mercy was safe. What Dan Dallobar wanted now was Abe Teegle and the railroad money. Rip Colen wanted Teegle too, but for a different reason. He said the money didn't matter any more. None of them had questioned Mercy about her relationship with Teegle which obviously, while they'd been in Ma's place, had been completely respectable.

Madam Grace went out into the kitchen to get the big coffee-pot off the stove: everybody wanted a refill.

After what had been happening lately the back door should have been locked. But it wasn't. A man came through the door into the lighted expanse, gun in hand, and was as startled at seeing Grace as she was to see him.

Grace, never a backward-thinking lady, threw the coffee-pot at the intruder. And then she screamed, a penetrating banshee sound.

The coffee-pot caught the intruder in the chest, causing him to drop his gun. He yowled as the hot liquid spilled down him, right through to his crotch. Grace charged forward and kicked him in the same place with the pointed shoes which she'd donned before going on her *pasear* in search of Dallobar and his two sidekicks.

The man slumped forward. Grace grabbed the coffee-pot from the floor and brought it down hard on the nodding head, crumpling the hat, knocking it to the floor where its owner joined it and became still.

Dan Dallobar, gun in hand, came through the kitchen door. He must have heard something. The outer door was still open and another man came through it, gun in hand, gave a startled glance at the still body on the floor, and raised his weapon.

Dan levelled his Colt, thumbed the hammer. The bullet took the second man just above the bridge of his nose, bored through his face and out back, the impact knocking him backwards, his heels kicking up.

His body banged into the door behind him, forcing it shut. He slid down it, his blood making a long, smeary passage.

Dan pushed the body out of the way, opened the door again and looked out. He saw nothing moving. He shut the door again, locked it, bolted it top and bottom.

The man was as dead as anything could be. The other one wasn't so far gone, but bleeding and unconscious.

Madam Grace stood looking at the scene, still, making no sound now. But she moved out of the way when Dan dragged the unconscious man into the passage where an eye could be kept on him, if he ever woke up and became half-way healthy again.

Dan put his arm round Grace's shoulders. 'C'mon, honey,' he said, and she let herself be led.

Rip came into the passage, almost shoved the barrel of his drawn gun in Dan's belly.

Dan barked, 'Watch the front. Send the Miner out here to watch the back.'

It was then they heard banging at the front as if somebody was trying to break the door in. Then a single shot, maybe a try at busting the lock which, contrary to her usual practice, and maybe expecting some sort of trouble, Ma had fastened tightly.

The Miner didn't need telling. He came into the passage, almost cannoning into Rip. Then, narrowly evading Rip, he almost fell over the bulk of the unconscious hardcase. But he didn't drop his gun.

'Dead body out there,' said Dallobar laconically. 'All quiet again so far, but keep watch.'

'Right, Dan.'

Had they all partly expected something like this, Dallobar wondered? He followed Rip into the main room which looked out into the street.

Grace was already with the other two women. Ma, crouched beside the window, already had a gun in her fist. Grace seemed to have gotten hold of herself. She said:

'I have a pair of pistols upstairs and some ammunition. I'll go get.'

Rip followed Grace into the wider hallway. He called back, 'They didn't manage to breach that door.'

'I had it fixed again a while back,' said Ma. 'It's as tough as a rock.'

Dallobar had moved over to the window, turning the lamp off as he did so. A faint light came through from the lamp in the hallway, but the tall man was soon in shadow. He looked out on the street.

There were lights out there, but he couldn't see much. Figures moved fitfully on the opposite sidewalk but seemed little more than shadows.

You couldn't shoot at the shadows, might hit an
innocent passer-by – unless Toler's boys had
blocked off the street. It couldn't be anybody else
but them. Dan hoped Bret was with them, leading them, hoped he could get a shot at the
bastard, although he didn't know the man very
well, had never felt any actual enmity towards
him before. After all, it was Abe Teegle he was
after, and the train boodle; that was his job and
he mustn't forget that.

There came a spurt of flame, an explosion, a
smashed window and a shower of glass, which
missed Dallobar. He swivelled round. The two
women, crouching, were both unhurt.

Dallobar broke more glass with the barrel of
his gun and levelled into the darkness, to the
shadows where the flame had spurted briefly. He
thumbed the hammer. Over there somebody
shouted a curse. He hoped whoever it was had
something to shout about.

Those sonsabitches thought they had this
place under siege. Did they know that one of their
number was dead out back and another maybe
near to that? Anyway, the Miner would make
sure the second one wouldn't be able to put his
two cents in any more.

Grace came back with her matched Remington
pistols. 'I've loaded 'em both an' I've got plenty
ammunition.'

From the hallway Rip called, 'There's a small

window here, prime. I can cover here an' watch the door.'

Mercy rose, hesitated, looked at Dallobar who said, 'Join him, gal.'

She nodded. Gun in hand, she went through the door.

Grace joined Dallobar at the other side of the wide living-room window.

Ma, strong despite her years, dragged a stout *chaise-longue* across the floor.

'Keep low, Ma,' said Dallobar.

She grunted something unintelligible at him. She crouched down and, with a final push, had the furniture beneath the window. Then she grinned and said clearly, 'I'm with you, big feller.' She lifted her heavy Colt in her wrinkled fist.

There was a barrage from across the street and the trio got lower, kept their heads down against the showering glass. Curtains blew in their faces. There wasn't much glass left.

They opened up then, put down a barrage themselves, Ma's lips moving, twisting, as she cursed; Grace letting out a sort of Indian whoop.

There was a lull again. Dallobar turned away from the window, went in a stoop over the room, checked in the hall as Mercy and her brother opened up, one at each side of the smaller window where there was, however, room for both of them.

Rip's face was bleeding. Mercy was unscathed. Dallobar retreated, went into the kitchen.

'Want any help, Dan?' the Miner asked. 'The folks all right?'

'Yeh. You best stay here. I guess they're bound to try the back again. We don't know how many there are out there. Toler's got plenty boys at his beck and call.'

NINETEEN

There were Sharper, Tubs, the dapper operative Gilliver and his two partners; and 'Uncle Tally' and young Esteban.

They were going good – when something bad happened. Tally's horse, going at a gallop, stepped in a gopher hole or something, and twisted badly, throwing his rider.

Tally staggered to his feet. The other men turned their mounts and Sharper shouted, 'You all right?'

Tally didn't answer, was obviously more worried about his horse than himself. He limped over to the beast, who was vainly trying to rise, but couldn't make it.

Tally did the only thing he could, took out his gun and shot the suffering animal in the head. Then he sat down on the grass with his own head in his hands, his gun lying at his side.

Sharper got down from his saddle and went on

one knee beside his old friend. Tally looked up at him with tearstained face in the half-light.

'I'll be all right,' he said. 'Just bumped my knee is all.'

'You'll have to get up behind one of the other boys,' Sharper said. 'Mebbe we'll be able to get another cayuse for you on a-ways.'

Tally joined the slimmest of the three operatives. And progress then had to be slower, with Tally still leading the way, still the scout and the guide.

They hit on a small ranch and Sharper was able to buy a horse. But, as they galloped on, they knew valuable time had been lost.

It was full night, and late, when Tally halted his horse, a frisky young piebald stallion and said, 'Not far to go now. Just over the rise.'

They went slower, more cautiously. They saw the lights, more of them than they'd expected to see in the deep of night. They heard a sound wafted to them on a breeze in the cooler night with no moon and stars that were high and twinkled mockingly.

An echo of sound.

'That's shootin',' Sharper said and spurred his horse past Tally. The rest streamed behind, Tally in the middle now as they galloped down into the small valley to Daybreak.

Teegle came awake, looked about him. It was

dark, but light from outside came through a barred window right opposite him. No use trying to get through that. Besides, he figured he was someplace upstairs, a storeroom maybe: there was a pungent smell, the nature of which he couldn't identify. Hs head thudded like a trip-hammer. His eyes were bleary. He closed them for a bit, opened them again, closed them once more, then, working by instinct, got slowly from the pallet on which he lay, fully clothed.

He even still had his boots on.

He sat on the edge of the bed and opened his eyes.

The narrow door was to the left of him. There were items strewn about this little room. He didn't strive to identify them.

He bent and took off his boots. His head thudded again. I heard noises, he thought. Did noises wake him up. The thudding didn't stop. Strange! He closed his eyes again but that didn't help much.

He realized he was listening to gunshots from outside in the night.

He forced himself to open his eyes again, forced himself to rise. In his stockinged feet, he went over to the window. He peered through the iron bars, through the grimy glass which had a crack down the middle.

There were lights. People moved around. He was upstairs all right. He couldn't see much. He heard voices but couldn't make out words.

More gunfire, though that seemed to be coming from a distance away, the other end of the street maybe from the Golden Calf where he was incarcerated.

He padded to the door. It was stout. Locked, obviously. He went back to his pallet, which was propped up at each corner with smallish containers that looked like oil drums, something like that.

He sat down. He put his boots back on. Then he lay on his side and began to set up a horrible agonized moaning which grew in intensity.

He kept his eyes closed, heard the door opening, the heavy boot-heels. He opened his eyes to slits. Gun in hand a man bent over him.

'What in hell...?'

The rest of his words were choked off as Teegle's hands closed over his throat, strong fingers digging into his windpipe. And a knee came up, caught him under the armpit and his gun was precipitated from his hand.

The gun hit the hard board floor. Teegle flung the man away from him, then bent and grabbed the gun.

The choking man, trying to get his breath back and rise to a sitting position at the same time, looked up at the tall man standing over him, gun levelled.

And Teegle said, 'I'm gonna ask you some questions and you're gonna answer 'em fast or I'm gonna blow your head off.'

With the lamplight coming in from the open door and the diffused glow from the window the fallen hardcase could see Teegle's battered face now. And his eyes. The eyes of a killer who meant every word he'd said.

'I ain't aimin' to die,' the man said, resting on one elbow.

'Where's the shooting comin' from and who is doing it?'

'Bret Toler an' some o' the boys. They're down by Ma Dodds' place. Dan Dallobar's there an' Rip Colen – an' – an' that girl who escaped.'

'Where did Toler put the money?'

'I don't know. I ...'

'I've no time to waste.'

'I guess he put it in the safe. And nobody knows the combination 'cept him.'

'Where?'

'In his office ... In his office.'

Teegle knew where the office was. He bent swiftly, swung the gun.

It was a savage, killing blow, which drove the man flat on his back, stretched out, still.

Teegle didn't give him another glance, went through the door. He didn't think he'd be able to do anything with the safe in the office. But, hell, he had to take a look.

Maybe he'd be able to make Bret tell what the

combination was. The thought made him grin, and that hurt his sore face. But he didn't think his head was aching so much.

The Miner had put out the lamp ages ago. At least it seemed like ages ago. He heard the shooting out front and worried for his friends. But he also knew that he must stay at his post. That was what Dan had told him to do and, for him, now, Dan was the chief – and he wondered what he had ever seen in Abe Teegle, the treacherous murdering sonabitch.

He sat in a wooden chair facing the window, his gun on his knee. There was a lull from time to time in the sounds of shooting which came to him out here like the popping of firecrackers.

There was a lull again and he was contemplating walking to the front to see how the others were faring: he was afraid for them.

Then he heard the sound from the other side of the window. He thought he saw a movement; he *sensed* it. He pointed his gun at the window and fired a shot. The window smashed with a louder sound than he could have expected, half deafening him. He slid from his chair so as to make himself a lesser target if needs be. His head sang. But then there was quiet.

Dallobar came in.

'You all right, old son?'

'Yeh. I thought there was somebody outside the window. I took a shot.'

Skilfully moving in the darkness and avoiding the Miner's legs as the older man drew his knees up, Dallobar went to the back door. He turned the key, shot the bolts. The Miner saw the gun glinting in the tall man's fist as, with his other hand, he opened the door a crack.

A rifle-shot sounded, followed by nasty whiplash echoes. Dallobar drew back with a small curse, slamming the door, moving aside.

'Way back. But no slouch. Nearly took my ear off.'

'Mebbe I was shootin' at nothing then,' the Miner said. 'Smashin' the damn window an' all.'

'Better than just sittin',' said Dallobar with a small spurt of harsh laughter. 'I was thinking of trying to get the women out this back way. But I should've guessed that Toler wouldn't leave the back uncovered, particularly after what had happened to his first two boys. The body's still out there. And there's the one in here o' course. I don't know whether that's a proper body or not.'

'He's no trouble,' the Miner cackled.

Dallobar said, 'I don't know what Toler thinks he's doing out front. Making a grandstand play I guess.' As he finished his sentence more shots sounded from out front.

As the tall man made for the communicating door the Miner said, 'Toler's the big chief around here. Nobody's gonna interfere with what him an' his boys do.'

Neither Dallobar or the Miner knew how wrong the oldster was this time....

TWENTY

Sharper threw caution to the winds now, leading his men fast. He hadn't meant it to be this way, had planned for a split up, a quiet entry into Daybreak where there was no welcome for lawmen of any kind. There could even have been a quiet meeting at Ma Dodds' place as Tally had recommended and where the Dallobar party might still be.

But there had been more shooting and it came from the other end of the town from where Sharper and his party entered. Here there were lights and milling people, for this was the hub of Daybreak. Here were the cantinas, a big half-canvas, half-clapboard structure that housed visiting and regular whores (a sideline of Bret Toler's, Tally had said), eating-houses, doss houses, a big bathhouse and, central to all those, Toler's Golden Calf, the gaudy palace of the king-pin.

We should have come in the other side, Sharper reflected very briefly, not sure. The shooting was coming from further away; from the 'other side'. Up here, among the bright lights, nobody was shooting at anybody. There was a cluster of people outside the Golden Calf. Others milled in the street. Everybody was, naturally, looking towards the area where the guns popped, the sound being half-obscured from time to time by the shouting voices.

Folks milled in the centre of the street. Sharper almost rode roughshod over a gesticulating old-timer; he reined in, his horse rearing. Tally, who was right behind his big friend, narrowly avoided a collision and threw obscene comments at the offending man.

Sharper pointed, shouted, 'Where's the trouble at?'

The old-timer, regaining his equilibrium, leered at the big man on the big horse, did a crazy little caper on spindly legs.

'Down at Ma Dodds' place!'

They went on.

'Spread out,' yelled Sharper.

The three young operatives ran their horses on to the sidewalk, scattering people. Tubs, Tally, Esteban and Sharper stayed on the street, but not so close together.

'Ahead,' yelled Tally, pointing.

Ahead there were not so many lights. And the

house that Tally had indicated was in darkness.

The horsemen began to close in. Shots were thrown at them from the shadows. But they had a great element of surprise in their favour. A man staggered into the centre of the street, arms out flung, and sank in a heap, became still. The attackers who had besieged the dark house began to split.

Tally leapt from his horse like a rodeo rider after a rough spell, scuttled along the sidewalk, up an alley that he seemed to know well.

He hit the back of the house and a rifle cracked, the slug taking his hat off. He dropped, clutched the hat. Somebody was shouting, sounded like an order. There wasn't another shot.

Tally eeled round the edge of the building. He knew this place, knew that back door, had used it more than once.

He hammered on it.

'Open up,' he shouted. 'We're here to help, open up.'

He knew he was taking a hell of a chance. But he'd always been reckless, foolhardy even. He was risking a bullet in the back, maybe the front.

But the door opened wide enough for him to get through.

'Sharper an' the posse are here,' he said.

Abel Teegle went along the sidewalk, keeping in the shadows as much as possible. Nobody took any notice of him. He'd heard what people said. He knew where his cousin, Bret, would be. As he left the Golden Calf by a side door he'd heard the riders out front. He didn't figure who they were anyway; he had other things on his mind, a drive, a hatred, no room for anything else.

The shooting seemed to have stopped.

That was kind of puzzling, though. Still he went on. He wanted Bret. And he wanted the money. He hesitated for only a moment. He fingered the gun which he had tucked into his belt. He went on.

The men came upon him from two sides. But it was as if they hadn't even noticed him.

Bret was the only one he really saw. They came face to face and Abe screamed his cousin's name and reached for the gun in his belt.

His was a fast draw. But this wasn't a holster draw, the kind he was so greatly used to. He snagged the barrel in some way at the top of his belt. Bret was faster. And his gun wasn't the only one drawn. It was the first to be fired, however: though Bret had never been quite as fast as his cousin, he had the edge now. Abe's gun wasn't completely out of its breech when the slug from Bret's weapon bored into his chest, knocking him powerfully backwards at so close a range.

And the three other men who'd been with Bret as a sort of bodyguard had drawn guns now and they fired them almost simultaneously.

Even as Abe was still on his feet, swaying, as if his hate was driving him, making him live, the bullets were thudding into him from all sides, spinning him, driving him finally off the sidewalk and into the dust of the street.

He was on his back, his sightless eyes staring upwards. Toler bent over from the edge of the plankwalk and looked down on him and said:

'Goddam you! You were family. I gave you your chance.'

His men looked at him strangely as they all went on. He pushed ahead. The main doors of the Golden Calf were now only a stone's throw away. They could keep off an army there. Other boys would be moving in from the back. But there had been dead left back there by the dark house where now lights were coming on.

There was no pursuit yet. The rough-riding attackers, led by a big man Toler had named as Sharper, would be checking with their friends. The Toler boys hoped some of those were dead too. Folks were moving to let them through. Folks were scurrying away, were beginning to figure things, didn't want to get in the line of fire.

The party entered through the wide batwings of the Golden Calf. There were not many people in there, far fewer than out in the street. A few degenerate barflies had been helping themselves to free booze. A fat man was slumped asleep over a table. An unshaven feller was trying to make time with a young whore from next door but was too drunk to operate in any way. And, when the girl saw the party come in led by boss-man Toler, she pushed the would-be client to the floor where, after hitting his head on the corner of the table, he lay recumbent.

'Out of here, all o' yuh,' Toler shouted.

There was an exodus, the young chippie running the gauntlet of slapping hands. Then some more of Toler's boys came through the side door.

The sleeping man was roughly awakened and kicked out. The unconscious drunk was lifted and thrown head first through the batwings.

Toler started organizing, giving out orders.

They were all there. Even the three women. Both Dallobar and Sharper had tried to stop them but without success. Even Tally's ribald comments on their presence had had no effect. Ma Dodds had said that Western women fought with their men and, as far as she was concerned that was it.

Dallobar said well, all right, but they'd have to stay back-up. He was already, with the assistance of Sharper, making plans for the take-over of the town and all it stood for.

The run-of-the-mill populace were not all stupid. They were disappearing as if from the pushing of a prairie wind.

And the law party would have to split up too,

in other ways, the women in the background.

They were still virtually together, though, when they came across the body of Abel Teegle. Mercy turned towards Ma and her friend, Grace.

'He was a bad man?' It was a question rather than a statement.

'He was, honey,' said Ma.

'He was,' echoed Grace.

Mercy's brother, Rip, was more outspoken.

'He was bad all right. A killer. He killed Bronc, who was his friend, who'd looked up to him always. He left me to die. All for that damn' money.'

'I … I'm sorry.'

'You don't have to apologize to me, sis. I'm sorry too. But, after all, I'm glad things came out the way they did. Dan's gonna speak to the Cap'n for me, so maybe I can join their bunch. Uncle Tally's gonna be with 'em and he's an old jailbird.'

Rip laughed, harshly, but added, 'But that venerable rogue is one of the nicest men I've ever known, I swear.'

'I'm glad you said that, pup,' Tally remarked, grinning with snaggle teeth.

This was an interlude. The luck had held. But death could still be waiting.

'Break up,' said Dan Dallobar.

TWENTY-ONE

It was strange about the townsfolk. Daybreak
was a pretty strange town anyway. Not the only
one of its kind, though, Uncle Tally had affirmed.
Not by a long chalk. And that old owlhooter was
the one who'd known.

Like most places Daybreak had started as a
settlement. Nobody seemed to know why, what
for. And even the original name, and it must've
been called something, had been lost in time, had
been Mex or Injun-like.

And this wasn't the first time there'd been gun
battles here, that was for sure.

Gunfire crackled intermittently. The folk in the
Golden Calf were sort of entrenched: the
pursuers hadn't been able to catch up with any of
them. Now the posse took over, their horses not
too far away. They hid in alleys, corners, a
disused outhouse, two of them in equally disused
privies.

There were still some ordinary townsfolk about. If you could call 'em ordinary. Peering, taking chances, bobbing up and down like turkeys at a shoot.

Not everybody played lip-service to Bret Toler.

There was an oldster on the sidelines. Older than Tally, older than the Miner. Sharper recognized the old feller as the one he'd almost trampled under his horse's hoofs when the posse rode pell-mell into town, himself and Dan in the lead, and Tally not far behind, like avenging demons.

Still, they hadn't done badly so far. The folks who had been besieged were unscathed except for very minor injuries. The three women in particular were prime. They could all shoot. Pity they couldn't see much to shoot at yet.

'Keep your haids down,' Sharper yelled.

Then the visiting oldster was plucking at his sleeve.

'Name of Moses,' he said. If the posse needed help he could get a bunch of his boys, wild rannies down from one of the big ranches, ready to hurraw this town.

Moses was their chuck-wagon jockey and they listened to him. Anyway, they were on their free time and loved to raise hell.

There were some townsfolk who'd join in too.

'I know 'em. Hell, I came from here in the first place an' I don't like Toler an' his boys ridin' roughshod.'

Sharper said Moses and his boys could stand back-up if needed but they'd have to take orders from him and Dallobar.

'I see'd him before,' said Moses. 'Yeh, we'll be nearby.' He dissolved in the shadows again. Lights were few now. Dim ones deep in the saloons opposite: Sharper stayed peering.

A shot exploded from an upper window; a lance of flame. A dim figure. Sharper raised his rifle to his shoulder. He pressed the trigger, felt the small, satisfying buck. This was what he did best. And it worked; a figure plummeted down, hit the sod, became still.

'Champion,' said Dallobar at his side. He had been listening to old Moses. 'But they've got pretty good cover in there, ain't they?'

No answer was needed. But as if to back up Dallobar's contention there was a spatter of angry firing from opposite. Slugs thudded into wood, splinters flew; tall Grace cried out in pain as her cheek was cut; but then shouted, reassuringly, 'A damn' flea-bite is all.' She triggered her Remington in protests.

A lull. An accounting. No casualties. A snorting restless horse, a man's reassuring voice.

But most of these nags had heard gunfire before, cheek by jowl as they were with fighting humans, men who did this sort of thing for a living.

Dallobar said to Sharper, 'I got myself an idea.

151

You might think it's kinda crazy. But it might work. Listen...'

The shooting had started again. First one shot; then two, three, four; a spatter from both sides, yellow spurts of flame, a sort of intermittent thunder, then the smoke, and the echoes. Folks took cover behind a horse-trough, a couple of wagons, the corners of buildings, a steel-bound barrel, behind half-open doors. And now Dallobar was moving along in the shadows calling Moses' name. The oldster came, crouching, to meet him, listened, said, 'Yeh, we can do that.' He had something in one hand that Dallobar hadn't seen him with before.

'What is that?'

It was like a short bugle but with an enormously wide bell.

'It's my cow-caller,' the old man cackled. 'It's what I use to call the boys to chow. They come a-runnin' or I want to know why not. No bell-ringin' for me, that's for females. I'll use it to call you. Right?'

'Right.' Dallobar returned to his friends.

Moses returned to his boys.

'I want a wagon,' he said. 'No hosses, just a wagon.'

It was easy. Many folks were keeping their heads down with their livestock, weren't bothering about pesky wagons. The boys chose one and, under the old chow-man's supervision, pushed it round back of the Golden Calf. Then they set fire to it and, crouching in cover behind it, pushed it towards the back of the large building, gathering speed on a slight slope.

Shots were flung at them – cagey Toler hadn't left his back unprotected – but nobody was hit.

The boys scuttled back into the shadows and, even as the flaming wagon hit the back of the building, opened fire, pouring lead at doors and windows.

There was no returning fire now: the riffraff were trying to save their asses. The back of the Golden Calf was blazing as merrily as a huge Thanksgiving barbecue.

Moses went round the corner and blew his horn. As the echoes died, he heard the spiteful snap of a rifle in the street. Sharper, he thought; not called Sharper for nothing, although he rode his hoss like he was a rodeo star with ants in his britches.

Moses blew his horn again and, on the street, the shooting died.

A few odd shots came from the other side. Then a voice rang out. Dallobar, Moses thought.

'Come out, all o' yuh, without weapons an' with your hands over your heads. If you don't make it fast we're gonna roast you both sides.'

Somebody else was screaming words but they were indistinct. The sound of the fire rose to a roar, the hungry flames devouring the clapboard sections of the building and gnawing ravenously at the brickwork.

Men were coming out of the batwings of the Golden Calf, some staggering but all, as well as they were able, with hands in the air. Smoke wafted past them; but they were limned against the red and yellow flames.

'Side doors in that alley, Dan,' Rip Colen shouted, pointing.

Dallobar had also anticipated this, starting forward, Rip at his heels.

Flames reached hungrily, but there was not so much smoke and heat at this end of the building.

Toler was in the alley, after coming through a door which he'd often used. He carried the loaded gunny sacks and backing him was a big roustabout who'd always been the boss's favourite bodyguard. It was he who drew and fired.

The bullet whistled over Dallobar's head and bored into Rip's shoulder, spinning him, causing him to drop his weapon.

Toler dropped his burden, pulled his gun. The bodyguard was still on his feet but was toppling like a felled tree, a bullet in the side of his head from Dallobar's speedily-drawn Navy Colt.

Toler fired but he'd been too quick. The bullet went past Dallobar, missed Rip also, who was, leaning against the wall, his gun in his other hand; but now Dallobar was in this younker's line of fire, was protecting him in fact, crouching now, thumbing the hammer of the big gun. And Toler was staggering as if caught by a furious wind.

His weapon, gleaming redly, spun in the air, hit the wall, fell to the dust.

Toler screamed.

A scream of frustration, which became a whimper of death as he fell upon the gold he had coveted so much; and became still.

Dallobar came the few steps forward, avoiding the corpse of the big bodyguard. He pushed the fancy saloonman's body with the toe of his boot. Eyes, gleaming redly, stared up at him unseeing.

Dallobar turned away, bent and picked up the gunny sacks, stepped back to Rip, who was grimacing, eyes red, teeth red.

Timber crackled. It was becoming very hot and dangerous in the alley. Dallobar helped his young friend out of there.

'Went right through,' Rip said. 'It'll be all right.'

Uncle Tally came towards them, hobbling a bit but unhurt.

Old Moses was blowing his horn again. With glee. Doing a little caper. Two of his young friends, who looked what they were, wild rannies, were clapping their hands in time.

Lights were going on in the rest of the street. Buckets sloshing with water were being passed from hand to hand. There was a striving to keep the fire from spreading further.

Ma Dodds moved forward in the red light, the swirling smoke. Her friend, Grace, limped beside her. The heel of her shoe had been shot off, but the cut she had earlier gotten on her face was healed; only a finger of blood marred the worn face that had once been beautiful.

The lovely face of the younger woman, Mercy, streamed with tears as she approached her brother, who said, 'I'll be all right, sis.'

'Yes,' the girl said breathlessly. 'It's the smoke – just the smoke.'

Sharper was all right. Tubs was all right, had only lost his hat, which had been almost as fancy as Dan Dallobar's, that was still perching on the big feller's head above the smoke-blackened face.

The dapper operative called Gilliver had been creased on the crown of his head by a slug and rendered unconscious. Mighty untidy now, he was coming to, face smeared with blood; not as bad as he looked, though.

Prisoners were being roped together by the two unhurt operatives and Moses and his grinning cowboys. The old man had said that some of Toler's bully-boys couldn't shoot worth a damn, and maybe he'd been right. Townsfolk jostled the prisoners, menacingly, until Sharper bellowed, 'Back! This is law business now.'

A local woman brought forth bandages. Tally,

with help from Mercy and the other two females, did his best with Rip.

The young, wounded owlhooter was being looked after like a sick calf.

The Golden Calf, enshrouded in smoke, and spitting red flames at intervals, was beginning to fall. Wounded were being helped....

The local undertaker was already in attendance. At Sharper's insistence the man quickly covered the bodies of Bret Toler and Abel Teegle, cousins in conflict, now side by side: the last thing. Moses was blowing his horn again; but it didn't sound like a bugle. There was no shouting now, just the noises of crackling and hissing timber above which the hum of voices sounded like a dirge.

Here would be a goodness, though, some folks said. A change....

A new town. But maybe with the same old name.

But Daybreak would never see a night like this again....